D1440867

lock.stock
& two smoking barrels

Published by Blake Publishing Ltd,
3 Bramber Court, 2 Bramber Road,
London W14 9PB, England

First published in 1999

ISBN 1 85782 4156

British Library Cataloguing-in-Publication Data:
A catalogue record for this book is available
from the British Library.

Typeset by T2

Printed in Great Britain by
Creative Print and Design (Wales),
Ebbw Vale, Gwent.

3 5 7 9 10 8 6 4 2

# lock, stock
## & two smoking barrels

the novel

andrew donkin

BLAKE

# contents

For Helen Goldney
and
Ronnie 'The Boy' Fogelman

Acknowledgements

Special thanks to Ska boys Guy Ritchie and Matthew Vaughn for all their help, and Sophie Hicks for everything else as well as Stella Paskins for her editing, and Emma Chippendale for her reading.

# lock, stock
## & two smoking barrels

**prologue**

**london now**

THE THING EDDY did best was cards.

The sensation that Eddy loved most in life was the feel of a new deck of cards shuffling through his hands just as they were right now.

'Three card brag is a simple form of poker,' said Eddy. 'You are dealt only three cards and these you cannot change.'

He fixed his penetrating stare on the two potential players sitting around the small table with him.

'If you don't look at your cards, then you're a "blind man" and you only put in half the stake,' he continued.

The men at the table watched Eddy's hands working the cards as he awkwardly shifted the pack from one hand to the other like a real beginner.

'Three of any kind is the highest you can get: then it's a running flush — you know, all the same suit running in order, then a straight, then a flush, then a pair, and finally whatever the highest card you're holding,' finished Eddy, nearly dropping the pack mid-shuffle for extra effect.

'So you want to play?'

The two other men at the table looked at Eddy's face. One eye was bruised and swollen, it looked out of place in the middle of his young features, like he'd borrowed it for the night from an out-of-luck boxer.

Eddy knew that the odds of getting three of a kind in any one hand were exactly four hundred and twenty-five to one. He knew the odds of every single other combination as well because he was a natural, not just with the cards, but with the other players too. Eddy knew the tell-tale signs that spelt out the difference between someone bluffing and someone with the goods.

'Let's go,' said one of the men. The other nodded in agreement.

Fifteen minutes later Eddy was one hundred and twenty-three pounds and sixty-four pence down.

'That's a good hand. A flush beats my pair,' he nodded, over-sportingly. 'What about you?'

Eddy looked at the second man, who turned his cards over, revealing a run of spades.

'And here's me trying to explain the game to you two! Bloody hustlers! You're both hustlers,' grimaced Eddy, shaking his head.

The two men grinned; obviously they were better than they'd realised. Taking this kid to the cleaners was going to be a very profitable way of spending their nightshift.

'Okay, you got some real money?' asked Eddy.

The men smiled.

Another fifteen minutes later, and Eddy reached forward to scoop up the huge wad of notes and coins that waited obediently on the table in front of him.

'Odds chaps. You got to remember

the odds,' he advised, as if it was all an unfortunate misunderstanding between gentlemen. Eddy started counting his winnings.

The door to the small room flew open as a man in the familiar blue of a police uniform burst inside. He took in the situation immediately.

'I hope I'm not interrupting,' snarled the police sergeant.

The two junior policemen playing cards at the table with Eddy leapt to their feet, red-faced with embarrassment, and stood to attention.

'Comfortable, Edward?' asked the sergeant moving slowly across the interrogation room towards where Eddy was now sitting alone. Eddy ran his fingers through the wad of notes in his hand, causing the two policemen to twitch uneasily.

'Considering I haven't slept for forty-eight hours, that I've got a dozen broken ribs, a black eye, and I can feel a case of the flu coming on, I...'

'All right. All right,' interrupted the sergeant. 'Don't think that I wouldn't like to get rid of you, but before I can there's a little matter that needs clearing up. I've got nineteen shot, stabbed and generally mutilated dead bodies scattered over various parts of London. And what I need to know, son, is what the fuck's been going on?'

Eddy fixed the Sergeant straight in the eyes.

'If you think you're in the dark,' said Eddy, 'I'm in a black hole blindfolded.'

Then Eddy went back to counting his money.

# lock, stock

## & two smoking barrels

chapter one

london, nine days ago

EVERYONE IN THE CROWD was waiting to give their money to Bacon. The only problem was that they hadn't realised it yet.

Bacon reached into his suitcase and took out the last of the small bottles of perfume and carefully lined them up with the jewellery already displayed on the unsteady make-shift table.

The open perfume bottles at the front of the table were the real thing of course, in case anyone wanted a sample sniff. The cheap imitation stuff was hidden in the boxes where it would not be opened until the lucky buyer got it home and Bacon was long gone.

A light drizzle pissed down from above and Bacon looked at the miserable, soulless faces that streamed past without giving him even a first glance.

Jesus.

'All right. Let's sort out the spyers from the buyers. The needy from the greedy, and those who trust me from those who don't.'

A few faces looked over, alarmed by the sudden volume of Bacon's sales pitch.

'Here we go. You listening, ladies?'

A small crowd was now gathered around Bacon and his wares.

'See these goods? They never seen daylight, moonlight, Israelite, fanny-by-the-gas-light. If you can't see value here today you're not up here shopping, you're up here shoplifting.' Bacon was on and he was good.

The punters nearest him listened to his faster-than-light patter like rabbits caught in the headlights of a lorry. Quite possibly the same lorry that the perfume had fallen off the back of.

Bacon didn't pause for breath.

'Take a bag, take a bag. I took a bag. I took a bag home last night and she cost a lot more than ten pounds, I can tell you.'

His hand darted forward and picked up a gold chain.

'Anyone like jewellery? Take a look at that,' said Bacon, stretching it to its full length. 'Hand-made in Italy. Hand-stolen in Stepney. It's as long as my arm and I wish it was as long as something else.'

At the front of the audience, a young woman giggled loudly.

'Treat your wife. Treat someone else's wife. It's a lot more fun if you don't get caught.'

Bacon put the gold chain down and held up one of the sealed perfume boxes, displaying it to the audience like he was about to sell them the crown jewels of England.

'Tell me if I'm going too cheap. Not ninety, not eighty, not forty, half that and half that again. That's right, ten pounds. Don't think because it's sealed up it's an empty box. The only man who sells empty boxes is the undertaker, and by the look of some of you lot here today I would have made more money with me measuring tape.'

The final words had hardly left Bacon's mouth when a voice piped up from the back of the crowd.

'Bargain. That's a bloody bargain if I ever heard one.'

The crowd parted a little as a tall, thin, figure in a long brown coat elbowed his way through the bodies.

'That's right, sir, push through. Put one leg in front of the other,' encouraged Bacon. 'They call it walking.'

In the new arrival's hand was a collection of dirty and crumpled ten pound notes and it seemed that he just couldn't wait to get rid of them.

'Did you say ten pounds?' continued the figure, with all the innocence of a choirboy on crack cocaine, 'I'll have five.'

'Certainly, sir,' said Bacon, casually. 'I'll just wrap.'

He picked up a box of perfume at random and began dressing it up in some cheap gift paper.

Without any warning, Bacon suddenly turned his full attention to a woman in the front row nearest him.

'Sorry, sir, ladies first and all that,' he smiled, now holding out the wrapped box enticingly towards this new target.

The woman in question was a tourist rather than a local and she felt the crowd turn to watch her. Bacon had chosen well and she quickly started fumbling through her bag looking for her money. She found a ten pound note and couldn't have handed it more quickly to Bacon if the money had had a serious disease.

With the first box sold, the floodgates opened. Bacon could see ten pound notes appearing out of pockets and handbags everywhere. The crowd forgot the first enthusiastic punter and moved in on the bargain of the century.

'Buy them. You better buy them. They're not stolen, they just never been paid for, that's all. And we can't get them again 'cos they changed the bloody locks.'

This last statement settled things for any lingering doubters among the crowd.

'Too late, too late will be the cry, when the man with the bargains has passed you by.'

Bacon grinned and paused for a split second to savour the smell of the money that was being urgently thrust at him from all directions. Sweet.

'Who's next then?'

Bacon's hand reached out to grab the proffered tenner.

'Bacon! Rozzers!'

'Shit!'

The warning cry had come from the first punter, now suddenly much more familiar with Bacon. Every good street trader needs a plant in the audience, and Eddy was Bacon's plant. Bacon always said that Eddy could run fast, eat fast, play cards fast, but that when it came to spotting the roz he was fucking slow.

Almost too slow this time. Two policemen were barging through the crowd and heading straight towards Bacon's pitch like a pair of righteous SMART bombs on a mission from God. Tenners forgotten, Bacon swept the table display into his case and he and Eddy bolted in the opposite direction.

Almost too slow — but not quite. The police chased them as the pair headed towards the railway lines and safety.

They both knew this routine by heart. Bacon was called 'Bacon' because he had spent so much of his youth in the police station that people thought he was one of them.

Bacon, however, was a big boy now and, as Eddy kept reminding him, it was time to move on.

It was time to start making some serious money.

Nick the Greek was a huge blob of a man with a hundred weight of gold jewellery on each hand. When Eddy arrived at Tom's grocery shop, Nick and Tom were deep in heated conversation. Nick was pointing at Tom's stomach.

'Putting on a bit of weight, ain't cha?' he suggested.

Tom was undoubtedly one of the skinniest men in London, perhaps even skinny enough to be a supermodel had he been a very beautiful woman instead of a fuck-ugly bloke.

'What are you talking about?' Tom asked, pulling an even uglier face than usual. 'I'm bloody skinny, me pal. There's nothing to me at all.'

'Of course there isn't,' said Nick, with no conviction whatsoever. Then he spotted Eddy.

'All right, Ed?' he smarmed, extending his fat, sweaty hand for Eddy to shake.

'Nick the Greek, always a pleasure. How's business?'

'Can't complain. How's the cards?'

'Can't complain,' answered Eddy, completing the ritual.

Eddy looked over at Tom's stomach, making sure that Tom saw him doing it.

'All right Tom? What you been eating then?'

For a second Tom looked down and examined his nearly non-existent midriff; then he decided not to rise to the bait.

'Gentlemen, please join me in my orifice,' he invited instead.

He led Eddy and Nick the Greek through the shop towards his private sanctum in the store room at the rear.

Tom was the entrepreneur of Eddy's gang of four. He always had a couple of his dirty little fingers in a couple of even dirtier little pies. Nick the Greek, on the other hand, made it his business to have all twenty of his fat little fingers and toes in every dirty, bent and stolen pie in London.

Between the two of them there wasn't much they couldn't get hold of — at the right price.

'How much did you say the stereo was?' asked Nick, as they passed a shelf labelled 'Tinned Soups of the World'.

'You know how much it is, Nick,' responded Tom, barely missing a beat. There was already a grating irritation in his voice.

The store room was jam-packed with cardboard boxes containing just about every type of food and drink currently available on the planet. It was a grocer's wet-dream. A bright red plastic model of a London telephone box sat on the top of a pile of cardboard boxes, while around it lay smaller, even cheaper phones all made in the shape of cartoon characters.

'And does that include the amp?' continued Nick quietly.

'You know it doesn't include the amp.'

'Shit, Tom. I thought it included the amp.'

'Well, it doesn't. I can throw in one of these telephones if you like. But it doesn't include the amp,' said Tom, tossing

Nick one of the cartoon phones.

'Very nice,' admired Nick, before throwing it over to Eddy. 'Well, I hope it includes the speakers.'

Tom had just about had enough.

'It doesn't include the speakers, it doesn't include the amp, and it's not supposed to include me getting the hump with your stupid questions,' he complained. 'You want it, Nick? You buy it.'

Eddy watched the delicate negotiations between these two captains of British industry with great interest. Eddy took great delight in winding up Tom as often as was humanly possible and he could see that, to his great credit, Nick the Greek found it just as hard to resist.

'What else do I get with it?' said Nick, taking a drag of his cigarette.

'You get a gold plated Rolls-Royce as long as you pay for it yourself.'

Nick rubbed his chin thoughtfully, apparently rolling the deal around in his mind.

'I don't know, Tom. Two hundred seems expensive.'

'Seems? Seems?'

Tom had reached boiling point.

'Well this seems to be a waste of my time. This system would be nine hundred nicker in any shop that you're lucky enough to find one in, and you're complaining about two hundred? What school of finance did you study at?'

Pausing momentarily to draw breath, he gestured impotently at the air before continuing.

'It's a deal. It's a steal. It's the sale of the fucking century. In fact fuck it, I think I'll keep it,' decided Tom, working himself up into a fully fledged rant.

'All right, all right. Keep your Alans on. Look, tell you what, here's a ton,' countered Nick, reaching into his coat pocket and pulling out an enormous wad of notes.

'Jesus Christ!'

Nick peeled two fifty pound notes off the top of the huge pile and offered them to Tom, who, like Eddy, was staring transfixed at the bundle of cash.

'You could choke a dozen donkeys on that and still have enough left for a house!' exclaimed Eddy. 'Jesus, Nick, and you're haggling over one hundred pounds?

'What do you do when you're not buying stereos — finance revolutions?'

'One hundred pounds is still one hundred pounds,' stated Nick, calmly.

'Well it's not when the price is two hundred, and it's certainly not when you've got the national deficit of a small African nation in your sky rocket,' commented Tom. 'You are tighter than a duck's butt; now let me feel the fibre of your fabric,' he ordered.

His words hung in the air like dust in sunshine. Then Nick peeled off a couple more notes.

'You drive a hard and vicious bargain,' he sighed. 'I'll send someone over later to pick up the gear, all right?'

Tom escorted Nick the Greek out of the shop, then returned to Eddy who was still mooching around the store room.

'He gets on my fucking nerves,' Tom muttered under his breath. 'Give us a hand with this, Ed.'

The pair of them moved the box containing Nick's stereo towards the door.

'Bacon and I got lasered again this morning,' said Eddy as they made their way across the floor. 'The suitcase only bloody exploded open halfway down the stairs at the back of Woolies car park. We lost all the gear. Had to leave it for the rozzers or they would have had us.'

'If you want some replacements, Ed, you're come to the wrong place,' grunted Tom. 'I sell quality food stuffs and dodgy electrical equipment. You know that.'

'I know, Tom. But it's time.'

'Time?'

'Time.'

'What fucking time?' repeated Tom.

'Time for the game.'

The enormity of what Eddy had just said sank into Tom's brain causing his body to go into some kind of slow motion mode. The rights and wrongs of Nick's stereo were no longer important.

Tom led Eddy through the maze of boxes that covered every last inch of floor space in the store until they came to a gas cooker. He leaned down and opened the grill, pulling out the cooking tray inside. On it were five carefully stacked piles, each containing five thousand pounds in used notes.

Tom looked over at Eddy, the way a race horse owner looks at his prize runner the night before the most important race of its life.

'That is my twenty-five grand,' he said reverently. 'It's all there. It took me a long time to earn it, so treat it with respect.'

'Bacon's money is at home with mine,' said Eddy, picking up some of Tom's notes and flicking through them.

'What about the chef?'

'I'm meeting Bacon at the restaurant so we can sort out the chef. Coming?'

The chef, or Soap as he was usually known, was busy preparing a large chunk of the restaurant's evening menu when Eddy, Bacon and Tom finally arrived. Giant pans of liquid steamed away behind him as he carved up a meat joint on the kitchen's steel-topped work area.

Next to where Soap was working were the heads of two pigs. Their eyes were tightly shut, looking for all the world as if they were peacefully asleep. The only clue that they weren't was the complete and utter absence of their bodies below the neckline.

'And what have you come as?' asked

Tom, smiling at seeing Soap in his whiter-than-fairy-white chef's gear.

'Cupid stupid,' retorted Soap.

Soap was called Soap because he always insisted on keeping his hands clean of any unlawful behaviour and dirty work. He was proud of his job, and even more proud that it was all legal and above board.

A friend who hadn't yet had the pleasure of meeting Soap, once asked Bacon to describe the chef. 'A stroppy little sod. He's got more balls than a golfer, only he doesn't know it,' was the response.

Just at the moment, Soap had a bone to pick with Tom.

'That fruit you sold me, Tom,' he moaned. 'That's the last time I'm getting my supplies off you.'

'What's the problem?' asked Tom, who, having had the fruit in question in his store for well over a fortnight, knew exactly what the problem was likely to be.

'There were more small hairy armoured things in your fruit than there was fruit. You should run a butcher's, not a grocer's,' suggested Soap.

'If you will order stuff that comes from Kat-Man-Fucking-Du don't be surprised if your fruit picks up a few little tourists en route.'

'Little? Three of those bugs have ganged up and are now running the kebab shop at the end of the street,' said Soap.

Eddy smiled.

Tom lifted the lid off of a large pan of what would soon be Soap's 'Soup of the Day'.

'Oi, get your fingers out!' yelled the chef.

'I wonder if vegetables feel pain?' said Tom, staring down into the boiling water.

'We could poke you in the brain with a needle and find out,' said Soap, with his best-bastard grin.

'Never mind all that, what about the money?' asked Tom, returning to more serious matters.

Cool as a cucumber full of anti-freeze, Soap opened a drawer and pulled out a bag containing his quarter of the money. Being Soap's, the bag was made of neat, clear plastic and each of the twenty-five bundles inside were carefully tied together.

'There it is,' said Soap. 'When are you thinking of?'

'Tonight. Or if not then, tomorrow,' answered Eddy immediately.

There was pause of a second or two as this news sunk in.

'Are you sure you can afford twenty-five?' Eddy asked.

'Well that rather depends on how you look at it,' replied Soap, slightly alarmed by the question. 'I can afford it as long as I see it again, if that's what you mean,' he explained pointedly.

Bacon swung the black bag he was carrying up on to the table, unzipped it, and slid the money inside.

'You got the rest from Bacon and the fat man then?' said Soap.

'Yeah. From Bacon, the fat man and myself,' nodded Eddy. 'Altogether, that's a hundred grand.'

'Who's this "fat man" then?' said Tom, suspiciously.

The others ignored him.

'You want a sandwich, Bacon?' asked Soap.

'Can I use the phone?' interrupted Eddy, pointing to the small room out the back.

'Help yourself,' said Soap. 'So long as

it's not long distance to Australia.'

'No, it's short distance,' said Eddy quietly. 'To Hatchet Harry. I'm going to book us a place at his card table right now.'

Turning swiftly, Eddy slipped through the open door.

Soap, Bacon and Tom stood in the kitchen, only the bubbling of the large saucepan breaking the silence. Eddy was about to gamble one hundred grand on his much talked-about skill as a card player and it had suddenly become too late — far too late — for anyone to back out.

From the next room, the three of them heard Eddy dial the number.

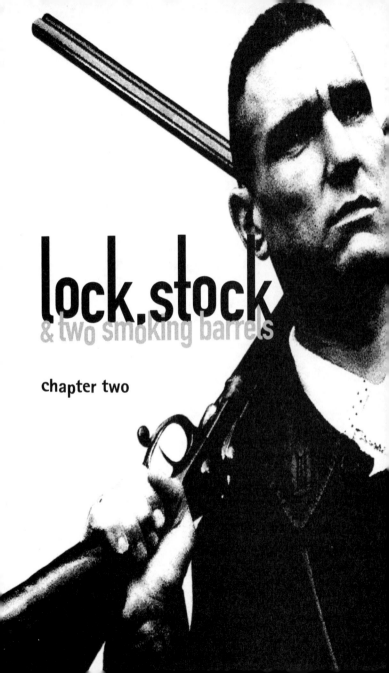

# lock.stock
## & two smoking barrels

**chapter two**

IF SOMEONE RAN a telephone poll to find out who was the most hated and feared figure in London's seedy and shadowy underworld, Hatchet Harry would, without doubt, be the runaway winner. He wouldn't expect anything less — the bastard would probably vote for himself. A few other faces would register, of course, but there was no one quite like Harry left in England's capital for pure, heartless evil.

Harry ran most of Soho's sex business, both the legal and the underground. As far as Harry was concerned, the more perverted and unspeakable services that his punters required, the more he could charge them for it. Sex and sleaze and antique shotguns were all deep and dear to Harry's stone-cold heart.

Part of Harry's trade was lending money; various-sized amounts to various-sized individuals. He had made his fortune long ago, and now if he was nasty to someone because they owed him, it was simply because he enjoyed it.

When Hatchet Harry was due money he always got it, one way or another. The ill-fated individuals in his debt were pursued by the best debt collector in the game — Big Chris.

One of the few things that Harry dirtied his own hands with was playing cards, running one of the biggest games in town. It was not easy to take a seat at Harry's table; he demanded a minimum stake of one hundred grand, but there was never any shortage of punters who thought they had what it took.

Harry was a hard-looking man in his fifties with a tight, neat moustache and well-kept, greying hair. His eyes were bright and alert as he sat behind the large antique desk in the centre of his office, with the telephone held close against his ear. The guy at the other end of the line was trying very hard to keep his cool.

'You got it all?' asked Harry.

'A hundred grand,' came Eddy's answer.

How come that skinny kid has suddenly got his greedy mitts on a hundred grand, wondered Harry. He ran the fingers of his free hand over his trademark desk ornament. It was hatchet resting in a block of wood, poised for use like a judge's hammer.

Still, if he had it, it was his to lose.

'If you've got it, you've got it. You know the house rules. Now if you don't mind...'

Harry abruptly slammed down the phone and considered the objects in front of him. To the left of the hatchet was an item known in the sex trade as a Monster G-Spot Tickler Dildo, and next to that was a Giant Bully Boy vibrator. Harry's desk was littered with sex toys of every description: from Japanese Ben-Wa balls, to turbo strokers.

Then he looked across the office to the leather sofa, where a massive, monster of a man was sitting.

Barry the Baptist. If scientists of the future ever succeed in crossing human DNA with the DNA of the ugliest, meanest, most-bastard Pit Bull terrier in the world, then the creature they will create will be Barry the Baptist.

Barry was Harry's right-hand man and general enforcer. His regular perch on the other side of Harry's office was arranged so that a visitor couldn't watch both Harry and him at the same time. It was a set up that had not only served them well, but had saved their nasty little lives on more than one occasion.

Barry the Baptist got his name from his habit of drowning people for Hatchet Harry. It was an occupation he enjoyed, and approached it with a commendable degree of professionalism. Barry used an oil drum for his drownings, strictly timing the period that he held his victims underwater. He was good at making sure debts got settled and that jobs got done.

'So what's this Eddy like then?' asked Harry at last.

'He's a fucking thief,' answered Barry in a low, rasping voice. 'He's been shaking the knees of a lot of good players in the park. Couple of weeks ago he took Sid the Circus for everything he had. Did him straight too.'

'So he can play?' remarked Harry, leaning back into his padded chair.

'The boy has a rare ability,' confirmed Barry. 'He seems to be able to make cards transparent. He knows when people are bluffing, and especially when they ain't. He's an exceptionally...'

'All right, all right, so we can say he is good, 'interrupted Harry.

'Better than good, he's a fucking liability, ' insisted Barry.

'So where did he get a hundred grand from?'

'Like I said, him and his cards have been scaring people all around the park. Won some money that way,' replied Barry. 'He's got some adhesive mates probably put up the rest. Names are Bacon, Soap and someone they call the fat man. They're like brothers — probably tossed it up between them.'

'And you're sure this Eddy is JD's

son?' asked Harry.

'Sure,' nodded Barry. 'And JD owns the whole property. No mortgage, no debts; lock, stock and sodding lot. That bar is his, and his alone. Don't worry, I've got it under control.'

'Good.'

Harry got up from his desk. Easing himself around a pile of brown boxes labelled 'Double Intruder — the Two-Timing Dildo', he walked over to the glass cabinet that stood against the wall behind him. Inside the cabinet were a collection of antique shotguns — one of the few loves of Harry's life.

Reaching forward, Harry opened one of the doors and carefully slid out a glossy brochure bearing the logo of Christies auctioneers on its cover.

'I've got something else for you to get under control as well,' he said. 'Take a look at this.'

Harry thrust the open catalogue under Barry's nose. The page in question showed a pair of antique hammer-lock shotguns in near perfect condition.

'It seems that some posh git called Lord Appleton Smythe has fallen on hard times and run out of money, poor old bastard,' he explained. 'These little beauties are up for auction next month and I want them. Only I don't want to pay a quarter of a million quid for them, if you know what I mean?'

Barry knew precisely what Hatchet Harry meant.

'You want me to make him a prior offer?' asked Barry.

'Exactly. One of my associates has given me an address and the location of these lovelies. Make sure we get everything from inside the gun cabinet,' ordered Harry. 'Everything. I don't want to know who you use, as long as they are not complete muppets.'

'You got it.'

'And whatever you do, don't tell 'em what they're really worth.'

Harry handed over the details to Barry, then took another long and lingering look at the hammer-lock shotguns displayed in all their glory on the catalogue page.

'I'll get on it straight away,' said Barry, standing up. 'I know a pair just arrived in town that might be suitable for the job.'

As the big man was leaving, a new diversion caught Harry's eye.

'Hold on, Barry. What do you reckon to these?' he asked, holding up a flat piece of black rubber attached to a handle. 'We're sellin' loads.'

Barry frowned. 'Err, very nice, Harry. What's it for?'

'Don't play innocent with me, Bazza. It's for spanking!' grinned Harry. 'The infliction of pain,' he added, bringing the paddle down on the edge of his desk with a loud slap.

At that exact moment, the infliction of pain was very much on the mind of Mr Gordon Westall, mainly because he had never experienced so much of it before in his entire life.

For the last few hours, Gordon's living room had become nothing less than his own personal torture chamber. His hands and arms were bound with copious lengths of gaffer tape and he was suspended upside down, hanging naked from the ceiling. To add insult to injury, an orange had been rammed uncomfortably in his mouth, preventing any dialogue other than a few grunts.

In front of where Gordon was hanging stood a large and intimidating man holding a golf club. This was Dog, an ugly flat-featured thug whose forte was administering pain and agony to his fellow man whenever he had the chance.

This morning, Dog and his gang had burst into Gordon's house looking for the drugs and cash that Dog believed were rightfully theirs. Gordon and his partner in crime, Slick, had bravely, but perhaps unwisely, refused to talk. Now they were paying the price for their silence. And it was a very high price indeed.

'Golf — the best way to spoil a good walk. Mr Churchill said that. Ball,' ordered Dog.

One of the gang leant down and placed another fresh, white golf ball on the tee in front of Dog, who stood back ready to take another shot at the hanging target of Gordon's naked body. For the last half hour, the terrified Slick had been used as a human launch pad for the golf balls. The tee was located between his clenched teeth.

Every ball that Dog hit brought the

steel golf club closer to Slick's already blood-stained face. Every stroke seemed to miss him by a smaller and smaller distance.

'Give me a five iron, John.'

'Certainly, Dog,' answered John, selecting and handing over the requested club.

'It's a dog eat dog world, Gordon, and I've got bigger teeth than you,' said Dog, firing off another shot.

The ball flew through the air and, with a sickening thud, smashed into Gordon's chest before dropping to the floor. A great deal of Gordon's upper torso was covered in patchy red marks, each one the size of a golf ball, each one evidence of a previous high-speed impact.

To Gordon's right, a weasely-looking man with small, nervous eyes watched the proceedings with close attention. Not the brightest boy in any classroom, Plank was always eager to improve his standing in the gang. In his own somewhat limited mind he saw himself as Dog's second-in-command.

Scratching the sparse, cropped beard at the very end of his chin, Plank looked at the pitiful form of Gordon hanging in front of him. Somehow, in the same moment, he managed to feel sorry for the poor bastard while wondering if he could persuade Dog to let him have a go with the golf club.

'Ball,' barked Dog again.

The same man bent down and carefully placed yet another golf ball on the tee between Slick's teeth. As Dog raised his club again, Slick shut his eyes with sheer terror.

As Dog took aim, his eye was caught by a sudden movement from the target. Gordon was moving his head, desperately trying to attract somebody's attention.

'I think your man's trying to say something,' observed Plank.

'Perhaps, perhaps not,' said Dog, unwilling to break the action he'd already begun. 'Maybe I should have another swing just to make sure.'

Dog took his best shot, and the ball hit Gordon just above the waist, sending the man into further contortions of pain. Then, planting his foot firmly on the centre of Slick's chest, he leaned on the club and nodded at Plank to remove the orange from Gordon's mouth.

'Yes, Gordon, is there something you'd like to tell us?' asked Dog, as soon as the fruit was unwedged.

Two hours spent upside down as an integral part of Dog's indoor driving range had made Gordon desperate to talk.

'It's in the fireplace...' he gasped, spluttering to get the words out from his cramped jaw as quickly as he could.

'Shut it, you idiot,' interrupted Slick from underneath Dog's foot. No matter how bad the situation seemed, he couldn't bear the thought of their hard-earned spoils falling into Dog's hands.

The human driving tee was abruptly silenced as Dog slammed the heavy steel club into the end of Slick's chin, knocking him unconscious.

'You were saying?' asked Dog.

'The fireplace ... Just pull it out — it's in the bottom,' gasped Gordon. 'Go on ... It's all there.'

'Take a look,' Dog ordered Plank.

Plank walked across the room to the gas fire, leaned down and ripped it out of the wall. Then he began scrabbling around in the cavity behind.

'Jesus. For God's sake let me down,' begged Gordon, beginning to wonder if he had done the right thing by talking. He needn't have wasted his breath — all the gang ignored him.

'Here, Dog, I think you want to have a look at this!' grinned Plank, holding up a clear plastic bag.

'About bloody time!' Dog nodded with grim satisfaction. Inside the bag was thousands of pounds in used notes, and an assortment of soft drugs in the form of white tablets.

Dog turned to the man still suspended from the ceiling. 'Looks like it's time to say goodnight, Gordon,' he said with a sadistic grin.

Sensing that something very bad was about to happen to him, Gordon started to scream. Dog picked up an eight inch army knife, and with careful and frightening precision, threw it across the room.

The ghastly noise stopped suddenly, severed mid-scream. The silent corpse twirled gently on its rope.

Plank looked at where the knife had fully embedded itself into Gordon's chest.

'Oh, Dog,' he said softly.
Another body to get rid of.

J looked up at the bright light filtering through the leaves above him and took another long drag of the joint in his left hand. For a few seconds, he imagined that he was in the middle of a huge rainforest, surrounded by tall, green trees on every side. He stumbled forward, uncertainly searching for where the greenery ended and reality began.

J was wandering through the small, artificially lit forest of marijuana that he and his partners were growing in their house laboratory. As he reached the end of the run of plants, one of said partners swam into J's bleary field of vision. He was performing one of the regular quality checks on their merchandise. In his white lab coat and with a test tube in his hand, Charles looked more like a scientist than a drug dealer.

'This gear is getting heavier, you know, Charles,' wheezed J, coughing slightly.

'Tell me about it,' replied Charles, not taking his eyes off the brown liquid bubbling at the bottom of the test tube.

'You know, I've a strong suspicion that we should have been rocket scientists, or Nobel Peace Prize winners ... or something,' insisted J.

Charles turned to his stoned friend, who was staggering out of the indoor foliage like a hopped-up ape-man, and watched as he tried to focus his eyes.

'Peace Prize? You're lucky to find your penis to piss with, the amount you keep smoking,' remarked Charles. Like Js, his voice had a strong, public school accent.

J didn't feel like arguing. In fact, he didn't feel like doing much of anything except taking another drag. He smiled, as if to admit that Charles had a good point, and lifted the joint to his lips once more.

Just then the doorbell downstairs sounded.

'Who the hell's that?' muttered Charles, annoyed by the thought that he might have to stop and see a customer.

Reluctantly leaving the tests, Charles headed down the wooden staircase which led to the ground floor with its huge oak entrance.

The way to the front entrance was via a huge metal cage which was built around the door on the inside. The cage had been designed to give the laboratory maximum security, while still allowing trade to go on. The idea was that the cage would be locked, confining any unfriendly or unwanted visitors inside it, rather than giving them free access to the rest of the building and the precious plants upstairs.

Charles stepped into the cage and opened the outer door. Waiting on the doorstep and looking very pissed off was an exceptionally tall man, with black curly hair and a dark goatee.

'All right, Willy?' greeted Charles.

'Does it look like I'm all right?' answered Willy. Under one arm he was carrying an enormous, plastic sack of fertiliser; under the other was an almost unconscious girl. On closer inspection, Charles recognised her as Gloria, who was clearly only defying gravity thanks to Willy's help.

'Give me a hand will you, Charlie?' pleaded Willy, whose unwieldy burdens were both uncomfortably dragging at his ragged brown jumper, revealing the grubby white tee-shirt beneath. 'Here, take hold of this. I could break sweat any second.'

Before Charles had a chance to act, they heard footsteps loudly and deliberately descending the wooden staircase and the figure of Winston came slowly into view. Winston was a serious, streetwise man and he did not look at all pleased with his colleagues. Instinctively, Charles knew he was in for a right bollocking.

'Charles, why have we got that metal cage around the entrance door?' asked Winston in a cold, calculating voice.

'Err, for security?' shrugged Charles.

Winston was close to him now, and his gimlet eyes bored into Charles skull.

'That's right, for security. So tell me, Charles, what's the point in having it if we don't fucking use it?'

'I would have used it, but it was Willy, and Willy lives here, you know?' explained Charles.

'Yes, Charlie, but you didn't know it was Willy until you opened the door, did you?' spat Winston.

'Chill, Winston. It is me, and Charlie can see it's me, so what's the problem?' said Willy, unwisely stepping into the argument.

Winston moved even closer to Willy and Charlie, and raised his voice to full shouting mode.

'The problem, Willy, is that Charles and yourself are not the quickest of cats at the best of times. So just do as I say and keep the fucking cage locked.'

Willy and Charles stood there in silence for a few seconds, pissed off at Winston's extreme tirade and feeling not unlike naughty schoolboys.

Winston gestured to the air at the hopelessness of his friends, then turned his attention to what Willy was carrying.

'What's that?'

'That's our friend, Gloria,' answered Willy, leaning a little to one side so that Winston could see the face of the spaced-out girl that he was supporting for himself.

'Yes, I know that's Gloria, but what's that?' said Winston, pointing towards Willy's other arm.

Willy sensed more trouble.

'Err, it's a bag of fertiliser.'

'I sent you out six hours ago to buy a money counter and you come back with a semi-conscious Gloria and a bag of fertiliser,' yelled Winston. 'Alarm bells are ringing, Willy.'

'We need fertiliser, Winston,' said Willy, weakly.

'We also need a money counter, William. We have to get all that money sorted and out of here by Thursday and I'll be buggered if I'm going to count it,' bellowed Winston, right in Willy's face now. 'And if you have to get your sodding fertiliser, couldn't you be a little more subtle?' he added.

'What do you mean?' asked Willy, puzzled.

'I mean that upstairs we're growing a copious amount of ganja, yeah?'

'Yeah.'

'And you walk home carrying a wasted girl under one arm and a bag of fertiliser under the other. The thing is, Willy, you don't exactly look like your average hort-i-fucking-culturalist. That's what I mean,' finished Winston.

As a parting shot, Winston gave Willy a rough slap around the face, then turned and marched back upstairs.

'We still needed fertiliser,' said Willy, quietly to no one in particular.

Sighing, Willy and Charles started up the stairs behind Winston, struggling with the twin load of Gloria and the sack of fertiliser.

On the kitchen table at Eddy's house, twenty-five thousand pounds was laid out in neat piles of a grand per pile. Eddy sat at the head of the table, deep in concentration, counting and sometimes recounting each pile. It was getting on Bacon's nerves.

'You've got twenty-five from me, Tom, Soap and yourself,' he bellowed. 'There's a hundred grand there to the pound, so why the fuck are you counting it?'

'Because I like to,' replied Eddy simply.

Bacon wasn't a card player and Eddy knew that he'd never understand. Eddy was about to go to war and every single one of these notes was a soldier to be used against the enemy.

Tom and Soap had joined Eddy and

Bacon at the house that they rented together. Although the rent was unreasonably low, the place was such a complete shithole that the landlord should really have been paying them to live there. Paint was flaking off the ceilings and walls, and in some areas the plaster had fallen away completely to reveal the damp brickwork underneath.

The place looked like a bomb had gone off in a junk shop, with damaged and rotting furniture laying scattered across the room. A moth-eaten dartboard, used for many late night games after the pubs closed, hung on the wall behind them.

Tom was leaning against the fridge trying to work out how much money he could expect Eddy to make him in the forthcoming card game at Hatchet Harry's.

'A reasonable return for twenty-five grand invested should be in the region of about one hundred and twenty,' he estimated.

'Based on what?' asked Soap.

'That's going on previous experience,' explained Tom.

'That's going on optimism,' countered Soap.

Tom opened the fridge, looking for something to eat. He pulled out a plate with the month-old remains of an abandoned supper on it.

'Whatever it's going on, it'll still be enough to send you on a cookery course,' said Tom, grimacing at the unpleasant whiff exuding from the plate. He returned it to the fridge.

'You're not funny, Tom,' said Soap from the other side of the kitchen. 'You're fat, and you look as though you should be funny, but you're not.'

Tom looked down and checked his midriff, just in case he suddenly had developed a huge stomach.

'Fat? Who are you calling fat?' he demanded. 'What are all these fucking fat jokes about anyway?

The lights hanging from the ceiling suddenly began to shake as a train rumbled past at top speed. Yet more flakes of paint gave up their tenuous grip and drifted floorwards, while the light bulb near Tom's head emitted a few loud sparks, making him jump.

'Jesus! It's good in here ain't it? Dead handy for the tube. Remind me, why the hell did you move in?'

'Because it's cheap,' answered Eddy, momentarily looking up from his money counting. 'Like a budgie.'

'So, what are we doing later?' said Tom, who was getting bored with just hanging around.

'We could go down the bar?' suggested Eddy.

'The bar? We've each got twenty-five thousand quid riding on you being sharp enough to cut Hatchet Harry, and you want to go down the bar?' exclaimed Soap. 'I want you to get some fucking rest!'

Just then, the sound of a van pulling up outside caught Bacon's attention. As the engine was switched off, he walked into the next room and carefully peered through a gap in the tatty curtains that were hanging in the window.

A grubby van was parked by the pavement and, as he watched, five men piled out. The driver was carrying a large holdall so full of something that the zip was nearly bursting.

'The tall, ugly one with the bag is called Dog,' said Bacon to Tom, who had joined him at his observation post. 'The one following behind with a face like a small rodent is Plank, for whom the phrase "as thick as two short planks" can only have been invented.'

The men entered the house next door, slamming the front door after them.

'Shouldn't complain though,' added Bacon. 'Dog and his gang are another reason that this place is so cheap. Nobody wants neighbours like that. They're about as friendly as a dose of rabies.'

'How d'you mean?' asked Tom.

'He means that they're thieving bastards', said Eddy as they returned to the kitchen.

'I mean that when they're not picking peanuts out of dog poop, they're ripping off poor unfortunate souls of their hard-earned drugs,' said Bacon, with obvious disgust.

'And how do you know all this? You been reading the ABC Guide to Gangster Scum again?' piped up Soap.

'I don't need to, I've got ears,' said Bacon. He put his finger to his lips to indicate that the lads should swiftly shut the fuck up. Then he opened one of the kitchens many cupboard doors and gestured for the others to join him.

Immediately, the muffled noises from next door got louder. Much louder.

'Not exactly thick, these walls,' whispered Bacon.

'No you prat that's mine,' said Dog's voice, carrying clearly through the partition.

'Is that it?' came Plank's response.

It sounded like some kind of money split was in progress and Plank seemed rather unhappy with his share.

'How many times do I have to explain this to you, Plank?' was Dog's reply. 'You find a job worth doing and you'll find your share improving. Do you have a problem with that arrangement?'

Plank obviously decided that he didn't have a problem because he made no reply. Or at least, not one that the eavesdroppers could hear.

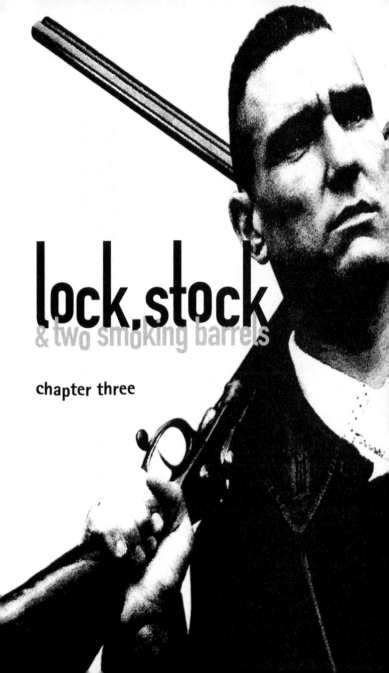

# lock, stock
## & two smoking barrels

### chapter three

JOHN O'DRISCOLL BREATHED in deeply and finally started to relax in the warmth and comfort of his sunbed. The last couple of months had not been easy for O'Driscoll. Thanks to a sudden and totally unexpected inspection of his betting shop by the powers-that-be, John had nearly been caught cooking the books to the tune of nine thousand pounds.

Only a quick telephone call and equally quick cash loan of very used notes from Hatchet Harry had solved John's missing money problem. The interest was as high as a kite on acid, but it was better than getting caught. And anyway, so what if John had got a little behind on the payments; it wasn't like Harry could take him to court, was it?

However, any court in the land would have been a much softer option than the one currently parking his car outside the health club where John was so diligently working on his tan.

Big Chris brought the car to a halt in front of the bright blue neon advertisement for 'Solarium Tropez'. Waiting for him in front of the giant window sign was his son, Little Chris. Big Chris settled debts for Hatchet Harry. The only thing he cared about more than an unsettled debt was twelve year-old Little Chris, his son and heir.

'How long has he been in there, son?' asked Big Chris, winding down the car window.

'About twenty minutes,' answered the boy.

'Is he on his own?'

'Yeah, just carrying a bag,' reported Little Chris.

'Did he spot you?' enquired Big Chris, trying to make it sound like a casual question.

'That nonce? 'Course not.'

'Good boy, you're learning,' said Big Chris, getting out of the car. 'Let's go pay him a little visit, shall we?'

Big Chris was, as usual, dressed all in black, with a thick gold chain hanging from around his neck. With the strong, square jaw of a sergeant major, he wouldn't have looked out of place driving a blood-stained tank across the cover of an issue of Marvel Comics' 'Sergeant Fury and his Howling Commandos'.

Having reached the second floor of the solarium, Big and Little Chris found themselves in a long, narrow corridor that was painted a sickly yellow colour. A series of doors opened off from it to each of the individual tanning rooms.

Little Chris tentatively opened a door and peeked through. He spotted a familiar bag on the floor by the tanning bed and signalled to his father.

'He's in here, Dad.'

Moving with remarkable stealth for a man of his size, Big Chris approached the sunbed in total silence.

'Sleeping like a baby,' he whispered,

hearing a soft snore emanating from beneath the heavy tanning apparatus.

Big Chris reached down and suddenly jerked up the top of the sunbed. Underneath, John O'Driscoll was naked except for a pair of thick black protective eye goggles and a small pair of pants. It was not a pretty sight.

John woke up with a sudden start as his privacy was so roughly invaded.

'What the fuck?!'

Big Chris immediately slammed down the top of the sunbed again, the full force of it impacting along O'Driscoll's body. Then he raised it once more.

'Mind your language in front of the boy,' he ordered.

'Jesus Christ!'

The sunbed was viciously slammed down again.

'That includes blasphemy as well,' Big Chris informed him, before once more raising the top. 'Now, tell me, John …'

There was never a good place to meet Big Chris when you owed money to Harry, but being naked and asleep under a sunbed had to be one of the very worst, decided O'Driscoll.

'Tell you what, Chris?'

Before Big Chris could answer, the door to the tanning room opened and a male supervisor wearing a white coat poked his head around the door, wondering what all the noise was about.

'I say, hold on,' said the man.

'I say, shut it!' snapped back Little Chris.

'You what?' said the white-coated worker, astonished to be addressed in such a way by what appeared to be a snotty little brat.

'He said shut it!' bellowed Big Chris, clarifying the situation by volume and extreme menace.

The man got the message and the door quickly closed. Big Chris refocussed his attention on O'Driscoll.

'Tell me, John, how can you concentrate on improving your lovely tan — and it is a lovely tan, by the way — when you have more pressing priorities at hand?' he said, leering down at O'Driscoll.

'Tell Harry ...' O'Driscoll realised his mistake, but it was too late and the sunbed came crashing down on top of him again.

'Did I say speak? And it's Mr Harry to you. Now, don't disappoint me and choose your next words carefully,' Big Chris informed him. 'You may speak now.'

'Tell Mr Harry,' O'Driscoll corrected himself, 'that I'll have it for him in a few days. I've been busy, that's all. I've nearly got it.'

This promise of future payment went some way to satisfying Hatchet Harry's debt collector, but it wasn't enough.

'Son, have a look in his locker,' Big Chris ordered.

Little Chris opened the long, metal door of the locker and started going through O'Driscoll's things inside.

'No chance of you lifting up the sunbed is there?' asked O'Driscoll meekly. His body was now running with sweat, though the tanning light wasn't the main cause.

'No problem,' said Big Chris, swiftly lifting the top up, then slamming it back down again immediately in one smooth, brutal movement.

'D'you want me to lift it up again?'

O'Driscoll groaned in agony, which

Big Chris took to mean 'no'.

Meanwhile, the twelve-year-old had struck pay dirt.

'Hey, Dad, he's not poor. Look, he's got over a monkey here, and that's just in his wallet,' Little Chris held up the thick bundle of notes for his father to see.

The boy looked at the man squirming on the sunbed. 'Fucking hell, John, do you always walk around with that kind of money in your pocket?' he remarked in his toughest voice.

Shock waves ran up and down Big Chris' features; there were some things a kid just shouldn't do.

'Oi! Next time you use language like that, son, you'll wish you hadn't!'

'Sorry, Dad.'

Big Chris turned back to O'Driscoll.

'Right, well we'll have that cash — all right John? You owe what you owe, and by the time this lovely tan of yours has faded, you'll want to have paid it all,' he advised.

Without warning, Big Chris suddenly smashed his right fist into O'Driscoll's face, like a striking cobra, knocking him out. He repositioned the top of the sunbed then turned the power control up to 'full'.

'Let's go, son. I'm sure Mr O'Driscoll would like some time to reflect on the error of his ways.'

Down at JD's bar, Bacon, Soap and Tom had spent the last hour drinking, and talking about everything except cards and money. They were now running out of safe subjects. The three of them had left Eddy at home, with Tom in particular insisting that he got his 'rest' before the game with Hatchet Harry.

JD's bar was a regular haunt for Eddy and the boys, partly because it was just the sort of uptown-downbeat drinking hole they were comfortable getting senseless in, partly because it was the sort of place that attracted good-looking women, and partly because the owner, JD, was Eddy's father. Owning that bar was the reason that JD usually had a smile on his face.

Bacon drained the last dregs from his bottle of Bud and put down the empty.

'Another round?' he said, looking around at Soap and Tom's faces for an instant vote.

'If you like,' said Tom.

'Well, do you want another one or not?'

'I don't care.'

'Since when do you not care about another round?' said Bacon.

'All right, I'll have another round, okay?' said Tom, glancing at his watch. He looked up again and saw that Bacon and Soap had seen him clock-watching. 'The only thing that I really care about right now is that Eddy gets some rest.'

'You're all heart, Tom,' said Soap.

'Listen, Cooky, it's in all our interests that the man rests before he plays,' insisted Tom.

Soap knew Tom was right, though he wouldn't have admitted it aloud. Twenty-five grand was nine months hard graft to Soap and he wanted to see his money again more than he was letting on.

'All right, lads? How's things?' said a voice from the other side of the bar.

The boys looked up to find JD's sharp angular face smiling across the bar at them. 'How's it going? Soap? Cooking going all right? And where's that son of mine?'

Bacon opened his mouth to answer, but before he could emit a sound, JD had moved further on down the bar to greet some more regulars. Bacon suddenly felt his arm being nudged by Tom and looked towards the door, where a tall figure had just entered.

It was Eddy. He strolled coolly across the entrance area towards them.

'All right, then?'

'What the hell are you doing here?' demanded Tom. 'Why, what's up?' asked Eddy, all innocence.

'How about, my foot up your arse?' threatened Tom. 'You've remembered Hatchet Harry and a certain high-stake game of cards, I suppose? You're supposed to be getting your rest in, boy!'

Eddy's eyes darted sideways, signalling Tom to shut up, but it was too late. Seeing Eddy, JD had wandered back along the bar and was now well within earshot.

'Hello, son.'

'Dad.'

'Did I hear right? You playing cards tonight with Harry?' said JD, staring at Eddy with his piercing blue eyes.

'Don't be silly, Dad. I wouldn't have anything to do with that,' answered Eddy, sounding convincing to everyone but himself.

Eddy was sure that JD could tell he was lying, but JD didn't comment. He kept his eyes fixed on Eddy's for a few seconds more, then turned and strolled away along the bar without a goodbye.

'Listen, I think maybe I'll get that rest after all. Pick me up at nine o'clock,' Eddy said.

Then he disappeared out of the door, leaving the others with their empty bottles.

'What the fuck was that all about?' asked Tom.

Bacon and Soap said nothing, but exchanged glances.

'Well?' said Tom. 'What's JD got against Harry?'

Bacon and Soap obviously knew something. Eventually Bacon came to a decision.

'Okay. This isn't exactly common knowledge, so I shall expect you to keep this buttoned up, all right?' he said.

The lads got some more drinks in

and retired to a four-seater booth at the back of the bar.

'A good few years ago now, Eddy's Dad and Hatchet Harry used to play brag together, right?' explained Bacon.

'JD was a much better player, but Harry was always a real shit to beat,' continued Soap. 'After money had been going back and forwards between them for months they decided to have one mother of a card game to sort things out for good.'

Tom sat in silence, for once just listening.

'This one game went on for about two days until JD had lost everything he had, but that wasn't enough for Harry; he wanted more,' said Bacon. 'They played on and on, right through the night, until the stakes were a fucking joke. Then it came to the last hand.'

'Harry turns over his cards and they're next to unbeatable. He's done it,' said Soap, taking over the story. 'Everyone in the room falls over because they've all lived through the entire night, and they all hate Harry and want to see him lose. Only with those cards, there's no chance of that.'

Bacon chipped in again. 'JD just sits there and starts to weep. Actually weep tears. He's lost everything he owns in the whole world. Fucking tears start rolling down his face. No one can say anything. It's a real mess.'

He leant closer to Tom, before continuing.

'Harry, the old bastard, gets up and starts fucking dancing. He's laughing, and dancing a little jig right in front of JD. JD's in proper tears now and the scene is close to pathetic. Harry reaches down and turns over JD's cards because he's crying so much he can't do it himself.'

Bacon paused, and Soap took over once more.

'The thing is, JD's got three threes, the best possible cards, and the only time anyone in the whole manor can ever remember seeing them together. Well, JD continued to cry, only now it's not looking so pathetic is it? Harry was so upset, he actually had a heart attack and got himself carried out!' finished the chef.

'Jesus!' said Tom. 'I never knew ...'

'No one knows, and JD likes to keep

it that way,' said Bacon.

'So — this place?' asked Tom.

'The bar we're sitting in was what JD bought with the profits,' nodded Bacon. 'JD never, ever played cards again after that night. Eddy, however, is even better with a deck of cards than his old man and wants to prove it.'

'Hence Ed's licking his lips at the chance to part Harry from more of his money. And hence JD's wish that he doesn't try. That's what all that was about,' concluded Soap.

Tom looked at his watch again.

Only a few hours until the game.

As soon as Barry the Baptist laid eyes on them, he began to doubt the wisdom of his choice. Barry had arranged to meet Dean and Gary, known collectively as the Scousers, in the strip joint around the corner from Harry's office. Barry was about to dispatch them to retrieve the antique shot guns.

'Evening, Barry, drinks'll be right over,' said the head barman. He knew exactly who Barry was and had more than enough sense to realise the man should be treated with the utmost respect.

As Barry walked across the bar he caught sight of Dean and Gary. They were sitting at the table nearest the stage where a twenty-something blonde was gyrating her hips and much more besides in time with the throbbing music being pumped over the club's speaker system. The two lads were rivetted at the sight of the stripper, who was wearing a black-sequinned g-string and knee length leopard-skin boots, and was in the process of removing her bra.

The bra flew through the air straight towards the Scousers and landed on Dean's head. Dean and Gary enthusiastically burst into a little cheer and a round of applause.

'Scouse peasants,' said Barry to himself, moving forward and deliberately blocking their view of the performance.

'Oi, get out the fucking way!' ordered Gary, in his strong Liverpool accent.

'Who do you think you're talking to?' said Barry, his voice low and dangerous.

'Oh, hello, Barry. Sit down will you?

We're trying to have some of this,' piped up Dean.

Dean was the smaller of the two Scousers and looked to Barry like a small tree-dwelling monkey who had been clean-shaven for a special occasion. His partner, Gary, had a thin beard and fat cheeks. He sported a large demi-perm that almost doubled the size of his head, and his clothes seemed to mostly comprise of large metal zips.

Barry sat down just as his drink arrived from the bar. He took a long sip and saw that Dean and Gary's attention had wandered back to the topless dancer on stage.

'Right, where were we?' he growled.

'On the phone you were talking about shotguns. Do you mean guns that fire shot?' asked Gary.

'Oh, you must be the brains then. That's right, guns that fire shot. Here's the address and a map of the grounds. The easiest way into the house is marked as well.' Barry passed over a folded piece of paper containing the details of Lord Appleton Smythe's manor house.

'These better be right,' said Dean

pocketing the paper.

'Make sure that you take everything from inside the gun cabinet. There will be a load of guns; that's all I want.' ordered Barry. 'I'll pay you when you deliver. Everything else outside the cabinet you can have, it's yours.'

'Oh, thanks very much. And there had better be something valuable there for us,' said Gary, sarcasm heavy in his voice.

'It's a fucking stately home. Of course there'll be something valuable there,' said Barry disbelievingly.

'Like what?' asked Dean.

'Like fucking antiques.'

Neither Dean or Gary had ever been in a stately home in their lives, let alone burgled one. Antiques were a million long miles from their usual hobbies.

'Antiques? What the fuck do we know about antiques?' said Dean. 'We rob post offices.'

'And steal cars,' added Gary.

'What the fuck do we know about antiques, mate?' repeated Dean.

Barry's patience was quickly running out. 'If it looks old, then it's worth money. It's that simple, so stop fucking moaning and go and rob the place. And I want it done tonight, okay?'

'So who's the Guv? Who are we doing this for?' asked Gary.

'You're doing it for me is all you need to know,' said Barry, leaning forward. 'And you only know that because you need to know, all right?'

'I see, one of those "on a need to know" basis things is it?' said Gary quietly. 'Like a James Bond film?'

Barry had had enough.

'Careful, remember who's giving you this job,' he finished, glancing down at his watch. 'I've got somewhere to be so I'm off, it's all yours now. Call me when you're done.'

Not bothering to finish his drink, Barry got up from the table and headed out of the club.

'Fucking Northern monkeys,' he muttered to himself as he went.

'I hate these fucking Southern fairies,' said Gary to Dean, as they exchanged a look of mutual loathing.

Then their attention was caught once again by the movements of the blonde on stage. Dean just had time to smile before a g-string hit him squarely in the face.

Back at his home, Eddy was sitting in an armchair, reclining in comfort in the pitch-black room. A tube train rumbled below, shaking the lights and windows like a distant earthquake.

He sat motionless, his eyes tightly shut. He almost looked asleep. Almost, except for his right hand, with which he was executing a perfect and rapid one-handed shuffle of an entire pack of cards.

Eddy had been playing cards since he could lift them up, and once he started he soon discovered that he had a big advantage over other players. It was not so much that Eddy was good with the cards — although he was that as well — but rather that he was good at reading people's reactions, however subtle or well hidden they were. And everybody has reactions — especially when it comes to money.

Eddy's right hand continued cutting and shuffling the pack, skilfully and faultlessly. The cards moved faster and faster, until they were almost a blur.

A knock at the door snapped Eddy's eyes wide open. Bacon, Soap and Tom were back from his dad's bar and were ready to accompany him to the battlefield, like knights escorting a warrior king.

Eddy picked up the brown leather bag that he'd placed by the side of his chair. Its contents felt reassuringly heavy — just like one hundred thousand pounds ought to feel, thought Eddy. Then he opened the front door and stepped out into the cold night.

Eddy was dressed all in black and looked even younger now that he was freshly shaven. Only the two white lines on the collar of his shirt stood out against his dark suit.

The four lads walked in silence through the backstreets towards the boxing gym where the card game was taking place. Hatchet Harry always varied the location of the games. Often they happened in the back room of one of his sex clubs; sometimes in one of his storage warehouses, and occasionally — for what seemed the most important games — Harry used the old boxing gym off Whitechapel Alley.

As they approached the gym, Eddy saw that two of Harry's men were on duty by the entrance to the boxing club.

'Invitations?' said the first doorman, who had a round face as pink as a lobster.

'Invitations?' repeated Eddy. Eddy's invitation was by phone and had come from Harry himself. Who were these jokers to piss him around?

'Yeah, invitations. You know, a pretty white piece of paper with your name on it,' said the second doorman, straining the limits of his wit.

'Well, how about one hundred thousand pieces of paper with the Queen's head on them? Will those do?' said Eddy, pointing to the brown bag in his right hand.

'All right, but just you. The others can wait in Samoan Jo's next door,' ordered the second doorman, begrudgingly accepting Eddy's right to enter the building.

'Samoan Jo's? You mean the pub? Hold on ...' Eddy protested, but he was cut short.

'No, you hold on to your fucking tongue and I'll hold on to my patience,' said the doorman. 'No one but card players get in here tonight, sonny, and I mean no one. Clear?'

There seemed to be no point in any further argument. Eddy looked over at Bacon, Soap and Tom, and shrugged his shoulders. Then he stepped past the two doormen and vanished into the shadows of the building.

Eddy walked through the empty and darkened reception area into the gym, where he saw the other players were already gathered inside the boxing ring itself. The arena was lit to look as if a heavy-weight fight was expected to start at any moment. Eddy raised his eyebrows at the thought of climbing into the ring.

The entire gym had the faded yellow colour of a newspaper that has been left out in the sun for too long. To his left, Eddy spotted a notice board on the wall, covered with the forgotten heroes and villains of yesterday. Leather punchbags hung from the ceiling in several places. Three thick ropes defined the boxing ring and the card table had been placed dead centre in the middle of it.

'This is a bit dramatic, isn't it?' said Eddy, taking in the scene. 'Is it supposed to be symbolic?' As he walked, his footsteps clicked on the hard floor and echoed around the hall.

'Evening Frazer, Phil, Don. How's it going?' greeted Eddy, recognising three of the men in the ring.

Eddy was the last of the five players to arrive. The others had already changed their money into the red and white chips that they would use to play.

'All right, Ed?' said Phil.

'Apparently we're using the ring for security reasons,' explained Don.

'I would've brought my gloves if I'd known,' said Eddy, now at the edge of the raised ring.

A grey-haired man standing in the far corner of the ring had been watching Eddy like a nosy hawk. Hatchet Harry himself.

'You must be Eddy, JD's son,' said Harry, watching for a reaction.

'And you must be Harry? Sorry I didn't know your father,' countered Eddy.

'Never mind, son. You might just meet him if you carry on like that,' was Harry's response.

Also sitting at the table was Tanya, a fading forty-something blonde who was acting as croupier for the evening.

'All right, Ed?' she said, looking over for the first time. Eddy had played in Tanya's company before and her presence made him feel suddenly at home.

'Evening Tanya, it's been a while,' grinned Eddy, climbing up on to the stained white canvas of the ring.

Harry's chips were already on the table and Eddy took the last empty place in the game. He lifted up the large leather bag and tipped out the one hundred thousand pounds it contained into a pile in front of him.

Harry watched him doing it and guessed, quite rightly, that it was the most money Eddy had ever had in his life. Tanya reached over and scooped the entire pile across the table towards her, exchanging them for the equivalent value in chips.

As Eddy watched his cash disappear, Harry suddenly knew he was going to enjoy this evening very-fucking-much indeed.

'If you are all ready, gentlemen,' said Tanya, 'then we'll begin.'

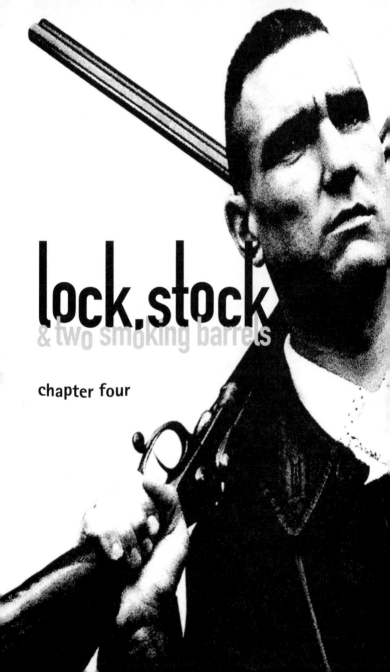

lock,stock
& two smoking barrels

chapter four

After Eddy had disappeared through the doorway of the boxing club, Bacon, Soap and Tom were left feeling somewhat bereft. They hadn't really expected to be allowed to watch the game; they all knew that Eddy, for one, would have hated that. Still, now that it was actually happening, out of sight and without them, the three of them were experiencing a certain feeling of loss.

'Come on, let's wait for him in the pub,' said Bacon, taking the lead.

The three lads sauntered down the alleyway until they reached the sign advertising Samoan Jo's and, as Bacon pulled the door open, a man completely on fire from head to foot burst through the opening. Orange flames engulfed his entire body and he ran off down the alley, with the lads looking on in mild shock.

'I heard this place was rough,' remarked Soap.

Once inside, they marched straight to the bar and ordered some drinks from the rather complicated menu. None of them had heard of any of the concoctions listed so they ordered those with the longest names — often a sound policy in a normal pub.

The place was decked out with large fake plants that hung from every available space. A television mounted on the wall was playing too loudly behind them, the football commentary drowning out all the other noise in the place. The lads were not impressed.

'What kind of pub is this then?' asked Soap.

'A Samoan one. That's why it says "Samoan Jo's" outside on the big sign,' said the tall barman, not unreasonably.

All three stared at the barman's bright

Hawaiian shirt in mutual disbelief. A man on fire they could handle, but this?

'There you go,' said the barman, putting the first of their orders on the bar in front of Soap. Soap's chosen brew came in a enormous curved glass and seemed to be ninety-nine per cent ice, with just a blob of green jelly at the bottom.

Tom's tipple arrived next; it was in a much smaller and more lady-like glass, and consisted of an unidentifiable slimy white liquid bedecked with several pink paper umbrellas. Finally, Bacon's drink appeared to be half a leafy pineapple floating in a glass of dirty washing up water.

'What's that?' he asked, gesturing at the monstrous collection of greenery under his nose.

'A cocktail. You asked for a cocktail,' replied the barman.

'No, I asked you to give me a refreshing drink. I wasn't expecting a fucking rainforest; you could fall in love with an orang-utan in that,' exclaimed Bacon.

'If you want a pint, go to a pub,' advised the barman.

'I thought this was a pub.'

'It's a Samoan pub,' said the barman, as if that explained everything.

'Well, whatever it is, get rid of that,' said Tom, indicating his tropical concoction, 'and get me a Diet Coke.'

The barman begrudgingly removed Tom's pink-umbrella number and replaced it with a more familiar glass bottle.

'Any chance you can get your man to turn the TV down?' asked Bacon, cocking his head at a cool looking black man standing alone in front of the TV screen.

'You ask him if you like, but I would leave him to it if I was you,' advised the barman.

The small dude with the large Afro and black suit didn't look very dangerous to Bacon. He had no idea that he was staring at top gangster and criminal overlord, Rory Breaker.

'Excuse me, could you turn the TV down?' Bacon yelled across the bar.

Rory Breaker did not react for three long seconds. Then he took a sip of his drink, looked over at the boys and said simply, 'No.'

The three lads turned back to the bar and in perfect unison said, 'Ooooh!' in their best impression of a high-pitched girlie voice.

Opposite Eddy, Hatchet Harry sat waiting for his first cards. His hands were poised either side of his body like a Wild West sharp-shooter itching for action.

Tanya shuffled the pack and began dealing the first hand, talking as she went around the table to the five players.

'As you know, this is three card brag, gentlemen. That means that three threes is the highest, then three aces and then running down accordingly; then it's a running flush, a run, a flush, then a pair. An open man can't see a blind man, and it will cost you twice the ante to see your opponent.'

Before anyone had the chance to even think about touching their cards, Tanya added, 'And don't fuck around, fellas; you all know the rules and you all know I won't stand for it.'

Tanya had a reputation for not standing for any nonsense at her table. Eddy, who had had the pleasure of seeing her working on several occasions, knew it was true.

As with all long card games that were going to stretch as near to dawn as the money supply would allow, this one started slowly and was in no hurry.

'Three hundred open. What sort of shirt is that then, Ed?' said Frazer, putting three chips into the middle of the table.

'One hundred and fifty blind. The type of shirt that has buttons on the front and collars at the top, Frazer,' responded Eddy.

'Three hundred and fifty open,' said Don, putting in his chips.

'Fold,' grunted Phil, dumping his cards back on the table.

Now it was Harry's turn. 'Three hundred and fifty open.'

'Three hundred and fifty open. You're the only fella in London I know who wears shirts like that,' observed Frazer.

'One hundred and seventy-five blind. That, Frazer, is because I am the only classy fella that you know in London,' Eddy informed him.

'Four hundred open,' said Don, nursing his cards carefully.

'Four hundred open,' Harry repeated.

Frazer decided it was time to up the stakes to something nearer a reasonable level.

'Eight hundred open. How do you like that, son?' he asked looking over at Eddy, the new kid on the block.

'When my knees stop knocking I'll try and live with it. Four hundred blind,' answered Eddy, putting in his chips.

Eddy had been planning his approach to the big game for a long time. He had decided to use first few opening hands to watch his opponents and study their reactions to every card that Tanya dealt them. He was already sure that Frazer had something special there but that Don was bluffing, and the next few moments would give him the chance to find out if he was right.

'So where did you get that shirt then?' asked Frazer.

Harry jumped in.

'Listen, ladies, this is a card game. Men play cards, you want to talk soft about shirts you should be at the fucking hairdressers, so shut up and just get on with playing.' Harry put his cards face down on the table. 'I fold.'

'All right. Two thousand open,' said Frazer, looking down at the cards carefully cradled in his hand.

'One thousand blind,' shot back Eddy.

'Two thousand open,' said Don.

'Swimming in the deep end, eh? I fold,' announced Frazer slamming down his cards.

That just left Eddy and Don. Eddy was a blind man and had not even seen his cards. Don was open and knew exactly what he had, but that wasn't going to be enough to help him beat Eddy, who sensed that he was bluffing on a very poor hand.

'Two thousand blind,' announced Eddy, out of the blue.

'You what?' Don couldn't believe his ears. Eddy had just doubled his bet on totally unseen cards.

Don looked at Eddy, examining his brow for a trace of sweat or nerves; however, there was no chink in this boy's armour. It was unnerving.

'Two grand? You're still blind. You've been eating too much English beef, mate,' complained Don, still unsure what to do.

'Well, you going to play?' teased Harry.

He was beginning to warm to Eddy's style. Not that that little fact would stop him taking the boy for everything he had, but he did like him. Don, meanwhile was feeling the pressure.

'Fucking right I'm going to play. Three thousand, there,' he said, throwing in the chips.

'Four thousand to an open man. You need double Eddy's ante, you know that,' Tanya informed him.

Eddy could see that he was getting to Don; he was really upsetting and unsettling him. Eddy loved it.

'Donald, do you know how to play this game or not? The reason I put in half the ante is because I don't know what I've got.' Eddy told him, needling his opponent even more.

Harry leaned towards Don as if he was about to offer some helpful advice.

'Fucking play,' he ordered, with all the helpfulness of a shark biting a swimmer's leg off.

Don lost the hand.

The game continued and the tone had changed.

Rattled by his own poor start and also by Eddy's jibes, Don lost hand after hand after hand. It was like a feeding frenzy, with Harry, Frazer and Phil all turning on him.

Exactly seventy three minutes into the game, Don lost the last of his money. He caved in to the pressure of his humiliating loss by climbing on to the table, in an attempt to annihilate the chips he'd been giving away all evening.

In civilised card playing circles, climbing on to the table at any time is considered bad manners, but dancing on your opponents chips is really the height of rudeness. Two of Harry's doormen were asked to escort Don from the gym.

'I want my money back, you slags!' shouted Don, as he was dragged away kicking.

The doormen threw him into the cold alley outside and bolted the door behind him.

'Wankers! Wankers!' screamed Don, but nobody was listening. Inside, another hand of cards had already been dealt.

Somewhere deep in the Essex countryside, just over two hours drive from the East End of London, Gary and Dean were arguing about directions.

'We should have gone left, you prat,' said Dean.

'We did go fucking left,' retorted Gary.

'Twice. We should have gone left, then left again. But no, you had to go left then go right, didn't you?' accused Dean.

Gary and Dean were poring over the map that Barry the Baptist had given them by the watery light of a small hand torch. They both knew exactly where they were — they were lost, but neither Gary the driver nor Dean the navigator were taking the responsibility for this cock-up.

'There's roads all over this thing,' exclaimed Dean in frustration.

''Course there fucking are, it's a map,' said Gary, before reverting to sulky silence as the two of them tried to make sense of the confusing network of coloured lines.

'Let's turn round and go back,' suggested Dean finally. 'We should have gone left back at that field that smelled really bad.'

'At this rate, by the time we find this fucking place it'll be dawn,' moaned Gary. 'We'll be the only burglars in Britain doing a raid in time for lunch.'

Letting off the handbrake, Gary turned the vehicle through three hundred and sixty degrees and drove back the way they'd come. A little while later he took the right hand turn that Dean indicated into a small country lane, and soon the headlights of the car illuminated a pair of metal gates with a wide gravel driveway beyond them.

'Fucking hell, look at this!' exclaimed Gary.

'Quick put the lights out,' insisted Dean. 'This is it.'

The Scousers parked their car and readied themselves for the mission ahead.

'No playing around with your matches this time, all right?' said Dean.

'Just give us a bunk up over the gate,' ordered Gary, ignoring the jibe.

Having surmounted the iron gates, the two Scousers did their best to creep silently up the gravel driveway towards the huge stately home that dominated the view ahead. In the expanse of the drive they felt exposed; anyone looking out from the windows could have spotted them at that moment.

'Why are we doing this during a flipping full moon, any road?' hissed Gary.

''Cos Bazza said it had to be done tonight, that's why,' hissed back Dean. Far away in the safety of the dark trees an owl hooted mournfully.

The Scousers reached the oak front door and paused as they got ready to pick the lock.

'Okay, Gary, we call each other Kenny, all right?' said Dean, pulling a black fishnet stocking over his head.

'All right, Kenny,' answered Gary impatiently. 'Shine the torch on the lock, will you?'

'Are you going to put your stocking on or what, Kenny?' questioned Dean.

'I've just spent one hundred and twenty pounds on my hair, if you think I am putting a stocking over it, you're very much mistaken,' replied Gary, shaking his head.

'You've got to have a disguise. You always have a disguise!' said Dean, becoming more agitated.

'Well I'm not having a fucking disguise tonight. Tonight, I'm just being me.'

'Oh Gary,' said Dean, visibly crushed by Gary's reluctance to don his stocking. 'You gotta have a disguise.'

The only reply was a sharp click, and Gary slowly pushed the front door open.

'Just follow Bazza's instructions,' hissed Gary, pushing Dean into the darkness beyond.

They tiptoed through the long hallway, but Dean wasn't letting up. Whispers of, 'You gotta have a disguise' echoed through the shadows until, to shut him up, Gary tied his stocking over his nose and around the back of his head. He looked as if he had suddenly grown a wild black moustache made of women's lingerie.

Gary sniffed at the fishnet stocking suspiciously.

'I hope your sister washed this before she gave it to you,' he muttered.

They had now reached a massive hall, where enormous gold-framed pictures the length of a man dominated the walls. Somewhere an ancient clock chimed out the quarter hour.

Dean shone his torch around the room, until the yellow beam fell upon a pair of beady eyes that were staring straight at the intruders.

'Jesus!'

Dean jumped back, then sighed with relief. The eyes belonged to a stuffed deer, mounted on a display base.

Gary picked it up and went to put it in their 'takeaway' bag.

'Put that back,' ordered Dean. 'We're here to get guns, remember?'

The Scousers made their way carefully upstairs and then split up to look for the gun cabinet. Dean was finally getting the hang of Barry the Baptist's maps and he found it first. The doors weren't locked so he opened the cabinet and began loading himself up with the old rifles.

As he lifted out the third gun he heard the sound of muffled screaming echoing along the corridor and guessed that Gary had found the sleeping Lord and Lady Appleton Smythe. Shaking his head slightly, Dean shone the torch around the cabinet, making sure not to leave anything behind.

Having carefully removed the rest of the guns, Dean carried the armful of rifles along the upstairs landing towards the only source of noise in the otherwise silent house. As he got nearer, he heard the sound he dreaded most: the sound of a match being struck. Dean quickened his pace and turned into Lord and Lady Appleton Smythe's bedroom, just in time to see Gary with a lighted match in his hand.

His Lord and Ladyship were in their four poster bed, trussed up so they couldn't move. Gary had inserted small pieces of tissue paper between Lord Appleton Smythe's toes and was about to ignite one with the match. It was something Dean had seen before.

'What are you doing, Kenny?' he snapped.

'Finding out where he keeps the money,' replied Gary, amazed at his partner's ignorance.

'Kenny, you twat, does it look like these people have got any money? Look around you. They can't even afford new furniture,' reasoned Dean.

Gary dropped the match with a curse, as the stick burnt down its entire length and the flame licked at his fingers.

'They might have something hidden away,' he argued crossly.

'Look, we've got the guns. I've got every one from the cabinet. Now, if you don't mind, let's go. What's the matter with you anyway?' yelled Dean, unable to keep what little cool he possessed any further. 'Every time we do a job you have to go burning people's feet. What's wrong with you?'

Suddenly, a tall, white-haired figure appeared in the doorway behind Dean. It was the Appleton Smythe's butler, armed with a pair of ancient hammer-lock guns. Dressed incongruously in a red tweed dressing gown, the old man aimed both of the guns straight at the back of Dean's head.

Boom!

Just as the butler fired, Dean lost his grip on the cache of guns he was holding. He bent forward to catch them, and the bullet passed through the space where his head had been only half a second before. The missile sailed over him and straight towards Gary.

The unexpected recoil from the gunshot knocked the old butler clear off his feet, and his bony body landed with a thud on the bedroom carpet. The second weapon in his hand went off, firing straight above him into the ceiling, causing a cloud of white plaster to cascade to the floor.

Recovering himself quickly, Dean rushed over and confiscated the weapons. The butler, who was stunned by his sudden fall, made no attempt to get up.

'You want to be more careful, old fella. You very nearly took my mate's head clean off,' Dean said, looking down at the old man.

If anything, the butler seemed slightly cheered up by the news of his near-miss.

'You all right, Kenny?' said Dean, looking across to Gary who was leaning against one of the uprights of the four poster bed. He was obviously in a state of shock, and it was easy to see why. It was a terrible sight.

The gunshot had torn through the centre of Gary's prized bouffant perm,

leaving him with a pair of smoking
Mickey Mouse ears.

'Oh, Kenny ...' sympathised Dean
weakly.

Back at the boxing gym, the stakes had
risen game by game as midnight had
ticked away into the early hours of the
morning. A whisky bottle, now nearly
empty, was being passed around the table
from player to player.

'Three hundred open,' announced
Frazer, putting in his chips.

'Three hundred open,' repeated
Eddy, glancing down at his cards.

Hatchet Harry looked at his wrist
watch and smiled to himself. It was time.

Exactly on the stroke of 2.30 am,
Barry the Baptist made his way quietly
into the gym's changing room. He sat
down in the middle of a collection of
discarded, sweaty towels, reached
underneath one of the benches and pulled
out a metal box. Inside the box was a
small four inch television monitor.

Barry leant down, plugged in the
power cable and attached a lead into its
aerial socket.

'Hey-fucking-presto,' said the big man, as a grainy black and white picture of the card table faded up on the small screen.

Hatchet Harry had chosen young Eddy's seat at the card table very carefully. It was directly in front of the gym's hidden camera. The camera was angled so that it looked over Eddy's shoulder, offering a clear view of his cards whenever he raised them to look at them himself.

Barry adjusted the camera's controls, first zooming in on the back of Eddy's head, then moving to the left and carefully focussing on his hands. At the moment Eddy was holding his cards face down, but Barry knew that he'd have to raise them sooner or later.

The screen suddenly faded quickly to black and Barry began to whack the top of the set with his fist.

'Come on. Not now please. Oh you bastard, oh you fucking bastard!' rasped Barry.

He gave it a shake and the grainy black and white picture flickered back just in time as Eddy lifted his cards up. Barry saw exactly what he had to offer.

'Shit. Two bloody queens!' he whistled to himself, then he picked up a telegraph-like device and began to tap in a code.

Back in the boxing ring, Barry's coded message travelled to a device on Harry's lower leg, hidden under the fabric of his trousers. Harry received the code that Eddy was holding a strong set of cards and said, 'I fold,' putting his own cards on the table.

'Four hundred open,' said Phil, continuing the hand.

Harry watched as Eddy won his third straight hand of the night. This kid could really play. Shame, thought Harry, that he has to lose everything.

Frazer, who had been struggling to keep up all night, lost badly on the next two hands and eventually had to stop playing when his money inevitably dried up. His exit from the game itself was altogether more dignified than Don's had been and for the rest of the night he could be no more than a spectator at the table.

The raised stakes continued into the next game.

'Ten grand blind,' announced Eddy as he received his hand.

Hidden away in the changing room, Barry zoomed in on Eddy's cards, but they were lying face down on the table untouched.

'Twenty thousand open,' said Harry.

'I fold,' said Phil.

Eddy picked up his cards and studied them. Harry watched his face for any reaction, but there was none — at least, none that Harry could discern. In the changing room, however, Barry had observed Eddy's running flush and typed in the relevant information to his boss.

'Twenty thousand open,' said Eddy, coolly.

Harry paused for a second while his mind digested the new information from Barry, then he said:

'I fold.'

Eddy's eyes narrowed. This was unusual play from Harry, not like his usual pattern so far this evening. As Eddy scooped his winnings towards him, he had a discreet glance over his shoulder, but he couldn't see anything unusual there. Nothing that should cause him concern.

'Don't go spending that all at once, boy,' advised Harry.

In the changing room, Barry's mobile phone suddenly rang, causing him to jump and nearly drop the television he was cradling in his lap.

'Cor, bloody hell!'

He pulled the phone out of his pocket. 'What?'

'I thought you said that there were no staff at that place, Barry!' came a strong Liverpudlian accent. It was Dean, who was currently standing in a telephone box in a small country lane.

'Did you get the guns?' asked Barry.

'You should see what they did to poor Gary,' said Dean, wanting sympathy not questions.

At that moment Dean caught movement out of the corner of his eye. Gary, whose near-death brush with the gunshot had shocked him into a zombie-like state, had got out of the car and was blundering about like a sleepwalker.

'Gary, get back into the car!' yelled Dean. Then, turning his attention back to the telephone he said, 'Yeah, yeah, we got 'em.'

'Good. I'll speak to you later. I'm a little busy right now,' finished Barry, and turned the phone off.

Dean, who was almost as traumatised as his companion, didn't notice that the dialling tone was now his only audience.

'Gary! Gary, if you can hear me, I think we'd better get you back in the car now, okay mate?' he bellowed, in case sheer volume worked. Then he turned back to the phone once more.

'Barry? Barry?? Fucking southern shandy-drinking bastard,' shouted Dean, whacking the phone receiver against the side of the box.

In the brief time that Barry had been occupied on the phone, the stakes in the next hand of cards were already rising.

'Twenty thousand open,' said Eddy.

'Jesus, my doctor would beat me to a heart attack if he knew what was going on here. I fold,' announced Phil.

Eddy watched Harry's reactions as he picked up his own cards.

'Got some cards there, eh boy? Thirty thousand. Back to you, Eddy,' said Harry with the rare smile of a hungry shark approaching a popular holiday beach.

In the changing room, Barry was hunched over the TV monitor, desperately trying to see Eddy's cards. But it was no good — Eddy's posture concealed the crucial information.

'Fifty grand,' said Eddy.

Harry studied Eddy's face. Was he bluffing? He couldn't tell.

'Eighty grand,' said Harry.

Eddy shifted in his seat slightly, and for just a brief second, Barry saw the hand. It was enough. Two sixes and a ten.

'We're gonna take you to the cleaners, boy,' he said, rubbing his huge hands together. Then he urgently tapped the information through to Harry.

'One hundred grand,' said Eddy.

'Hold on fellas, I know ...' Frazer started to say, but he was interrupted.

'I know you're not in the game no more, which means nobody cares what you know. Two hundred and fifty thousand.' said Harry.

This time, Eddy had decided to bluff it all the way. The difference was, this time Harry knew for sure that Eddy was bluffing.

Eddy and Harry stared across the table for several moments, minutely studying each other. A small bead of sweat formed on Eddy's forehead and began to run down his brow.

'That's quite a raise, one hundred and fifty thousand on my hundred,' he said at last.

'Yes. Is there anything else you want to say?' asked Harry.

'As you know, that puts us in an awkward situation. I don't have enough money to continue,' said Eddy, beginning to feel out of his depth for the first time.

'We'll have to see both your cards, if no one loans Eddy the money to continue,' said Tanya. 'It's a loan or we see both your cards,' she repeated.

No one around the table had that kind of money left and Eddy knew it.

'It doesn't look ...'

'I will,' interrupted Harry.

Tanya's head jerked around.

'You will what?' said Eddy.

'I will loan you the money,' said Harry, slowly and quite seriously.

The game had changed again.

The bead of sweat on Eddy's forehead was joined by another, and then another … and there was nothing he could do to prevent it.

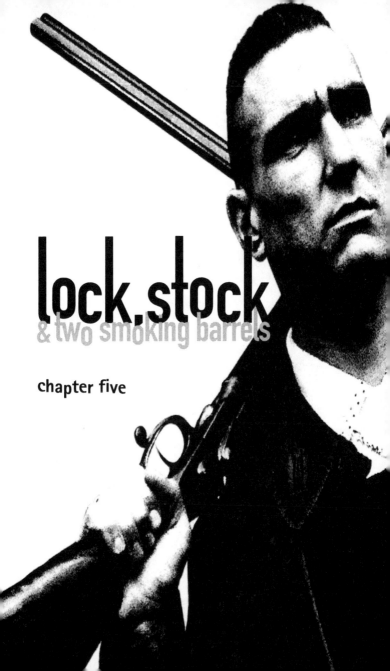

# lock,stock
## & two smoking barrels

chapter five

'I THINK I WOULD RATHER just turn them over,' said Eddy quietly.

Hatchet Harry locked eyes with Eddy.

'I'm not interested in what you would rather,' he insisted. 'I want to keep going. I'm offering you the money, so we don't have to turn them over because you can borrow.'

Eddy felt himself slowly drowning as Harry circled him, just waiting to move in for the kill. Eddy knew it, but there was nothing he could do.

Around the table, Frazer and Phil

shifted uneasily in their seats, hardly able to watch to brutal spectacle that was unfolding.

'I need two hundred and fifty grand,' said Eddy, unable to believe the amount of money he was suddenly talking about, and even less able to believe that Harry wanted to lend it to him.

'No, you need five hundred grand to see me,' Harry corrected him.

Beads of sweat now covered Eddy's forehead and his face was flushed with blood.

'That's if I want to see you,' said Eddy.

'Well, you're going to have a problem carrying on, aincha?' observed Harry.

For a few seconds Eddy froze, trying to decide between his two options. He could fold and walk away — that way he wouldn't owe any more money, but he was certain to lose the hundred grand he had come in with. Or he could gamble on his pair of sixes beating whatever Harry had — in which case he stood to win or lose a fortune entirely depending on if he could beat Harry's cards.

'You can still fold,' urged Tanya with

sympathy in her eyes.

Harry shot her a glance that said 'Keep your trap closed, you stupid cow'. Tanya ignored this and kept her pleading eyes fixed on Eddy.

Eddy made up his mind.

'I'll see you,' he said to Harry.

'For five hundred thousand pounds? Half a million quid?' Harry confirmed.

'Unless you're willing to accept my spare change instead?' tried Eddy.

'And he's still got a sense of humour,' smiled Harry. 'Okay, before I loan you the money I'll tell you what I expect if you lose. I expect my money back within a week. That's seven days. Crystal? Which means Sunday, okay?'

Eddy nodded. He was committed. Totally and inevitably fucking committed to the biggest bet of his entire life. And he had a very bad feeling about it indeed.

Harry reached down and turned over his first card: it was a seven. His hand reached for the second card and revealed it as another seven. For a moment, Eddy thought that the third card was going to be a seven as well, but Harry turned over a four.

They were terrible cards. A pair of fucking sevens. Terrible cards on which to gamble half a million pounds. Terrible, terrible, cards.

'Is that it?' said Tanya, expressing the disappointment of the rest of the table.

'He was bluffing!' said Frazer.

'Let's see your fucking cards,' ordered Harry, looking relaxed and nonchalant.

All eyes around the table fell on Eddy, expecting him, willing him, to turn over his cards and beat the living daylights out of the hated Harry Hatchet.

Eddy, of course, knew differently. Terrible though Harry's cards were, they were enough to beat Eddy's. His pupils contracted to the size of a pinhead while the world around him seemed to become a distant and irrelevant blur.

Fuck.

Fuck. Fuck. Fuck.

Eddy felt as if he'd suddenly been transported to a bizarre parallel world called Planet Screw-Up, where there was another Eddy just like him, but one who owed Hatchet Harry half a million pounds and whose life, therefore, was finished.

Like a slow motion action replay,

Eddy reached down and turned over his cards for the benefit of the others around the table.

'Jesus!' exclaimed Phil, as Eddy's fate was revealed.

Hatchet Harry grinned like a cat with a fridge full of cream.

'Unlucky, boy,' he said simply, already thinking about getting his hands on JD's bar. After all, how else could Eddy ever pay back the debt?

Eddy stood up, picked up his jacket from the back of his seat and threw it over his shoulder. He looked back at the table for a brief second then walked out of the ring on legs that had suddenly turned to jelly.

As he retreated, Eddy's mind struggled to come to terms with what had happened. Somehow the worst card player around the table had fucked Eddy like a frozen virgin with a pair of sevens. A series of blows to Eddy's head with a large baseball bat would have been preferable. Ten minutes ago Eddy had been thirty thousand pounds richer, now he owed half a million quid.

Sweat dripped from Eddy's forehead

and the nerves that had been so cool all night, suddenly contracted his stomach into a tight and uncomfortable knot. He stumbled, punch drunk, through the door and into the alleyway beyond.

How could this have happened to him? The thought played over and over in his mind. Eddy was good. He knew he was good. He also knew that his life was totally and utterly over. He had lost all of his money — and worse, all of his mates'money. Every penny was now sitting in Hatchet Harry's back pocket, while he waited on payment of the rest.

The alleyway began to spin around him. Eddy grabbed hold of a lamp post for support and doubled over. Sheer reflex made him open his mouth and he parted company with the contents of his stomach. The half digested mixture of chicken korma and whisky splattered on to the ground, splashing his neat black shoes and the bottoms of his trouser legs.

Eddy wiped his mouth with the back of his hand and staggered on towards the end of the alley. Without warning, a door opened in the wall of the alleyway and Eddy realised it was the back door to the boxing gym. The ugly round face of Barry the Baptist leered out at the young man.

'Hello, boy. Feeling a bit poorly? A little word in your shell-like,' he rasped.

Eddy did as he was told. He was in no state to put up an argument with anyone, let alone Barry the Baptist.

'Listen, I know that your three friends are responsible for a lot of that cash, so that makes them responsible for the debt too,' Barry informed him. 'You've got a week to find the money. After that, I'll take a finger off each of you for every day that passes without payment, okay? And when you've all run out of digits, then, who knows — maybe your dad's bar?'

Eddy didn't say anything.

'All right, my son?' finished Barry, shutting the door and throwing the alley into darkness once more.

As Barry's message slowly filtered into Eddy's semi-paralysed brain, the nausea built up and he vomited once more. Then, looking up, he managed to focus on the sign advertising Samoan Jo's bar at the very end of the alley and staggered towards it.

Inside the bar, Bacon, Soap and Tom were waiting for any dispatches from the war zone. They had passed an unsatisfactory few hours in there, surrounded by the tacky plastic plants. Thoughts of Eddy and the card game had loomed too large in their minds for any enjoyment of the evening.

Alerted by the loud shouts of 'Wanker!' at about 1.30 am, Soap had checked outside and seen, to his delight, the sad figure of Don trudging away.

'That's one down,' said Bacon cheerily when Soap reported the good news, and the lads had toasted Don's downfall.

'He's going to bloody do it,' said Tom. 'He really is.'

But after the unexpected excitement of Don's exit, the evening seemed to pass progressively slowly.

Until now.

Bacon saw Eddy first. He knew at once that things had gone badly. He had no idea how badly of course, but the Eddy that had just staggered into Samoan Jo's looked like one of the walking dead.

Tom was crashed out with his head

resting on the hard wood of the bar. Soap, having finished his twelfth orange juice was just sitting, staring blankly into space. Only Bacon remained alert. He sat between the other two, turning his silver flip-top lighter over and over in the palm of his hand.

'This doesn't look good,' said Bacon, nudging Tom with his elbow to wake him up.

'How'd it go?' asked Tom immediately, rubbing his eyes. Then he too took a look at Eddy and knew.

Still in a state of shock, Eddy looked at his mates and was unable to do much more than nod.

'How much of it did we lose? We lost half of it?' asked Soap, unable to entertain the idea of anything worse. Eddy's silence did nothing to allay his fears.

'We lost three quarters? We lost ... everything?' he said, his voice trailing off.

'Worse,' whispered Eddy eventually.

Soap smiled a genuine, uncomprehending smile.

'What could be worse than losing all of it? It's not like ...' again his voice trailed away to nothing as he realised the bigger possibilities for disaster.

'How much?' said Bacon, calmly to Eddy.

'How much what?' demanded Tom, who hadn't yet caught on.

'How much do we owe Harry?' said Bacon, gently but firmly to Eddy.

'Half.'

'Half what you went in with?' tried Tom, puzzled.

'Eddy, mate, are you all right?' said Soap.

''Course he's not fucking all right. Does he look fucking all right?' exploded Bacon, suddenly irritated by the other two. Only he understood what Eddy meant.

'We ...' said Eddy.

'Yeah?'

'Owe Harry ...'

'Yeah?'

'Half ...'

'Yeah ...'

'A million quid. And if it's all the same ... he'd like it by next Sunday, thanks very much,' finished Eddy, collapsing against the wall.

Now he'd finally found his tongue, Eddy let the others have it, in all its gory detail. He explained how Hatchet Harry was going to start sizing up all their fingers in a week. He told them that Harry knew that Eddy could not have raised the hundred grand he'd gone in with on his own, and that Harry saw it as their money on the table so it was also their debt off the table. Eddy hated to admit it, even to himself, but he could have kissed the old bastard for that. If Eddy said he wanted to settle the debt on his own he would have been lying.

'Listen, I wish to Jesus he would let me settle the debt on my own,' said Eddy.

Tom suddenly dropped his drink and made a half-hearted attempt to rush Eddy.

'I'll kill him!' he shouted.

He didn't get far, because Bacon blocked his path.

'Stop fucking about, Tom, and think,' said Bacon intercepting the lunge.

'Jesus!' Tom shook his head.

'Everyone stop dicking around and think about what we're going to do,' ordered Bacon.

While Tom had been reduced to

wild panic, Soap was developing his own special reaction: he was in a right strop. Not with Eddy, but with Harry himself.

'Listen, what's all the fuss about Harry? Why don't we just boycott the payment?' suggested the chef, to incredulous looks from the others.

'Boycott? Boycott the payments?' repeated Tom, in disbelief. He shook his head, 'I'm going for a piss.'

Soap saw that Bacon was looking at him as if he were insane.

'Well, couldn't we?'

'Let me tell you a little story about Hatchet Harry, shall I?' invited Bacon. 'Once upon a time there was this geezer called Smithy Robinson who worked for Harry. He had the biggest beer belly outside of a Sumo wrestling ring. Somehow, rumours started going around the park that old Smithy was on the take, so Harry invited him round to his office for an explanation. Smithy didn't see why he should have to explain anything and he didn't do a very good job.'

Tom had emerged from the Gents and took up the story. 'Within a minute, Harry had lost his temper and reached for the nearest thing at hand to use as a weapon. It happened to be a fifteen-inch black rubber dildo, and he proceeded to batter poor Smithy to death with it.'

'And that,' said Bacon, whispering right into Soap's ear, 'was seen as a pleasant way to go ... Hence, Hatchet Harry is a man you pay if you owe.'

Soap decided to take the hint that boycotting the payment might not be such a healthy option after all.

'Don't worry,' said Eddy weakly, with all the confidence of a condemned man who can already feel the rope around his neck, 'I'll think of something.'

The four lads left the pub and walked out into the light of a grim new day.

J picked up another fifty pound note and placed it lovingly on the ironing board. Then he took the iron and began to carefully work on the pressing the note perfectly flat. Behind J was the tall forest of marijuana plants growing upwards towards their own fake electric sun.

'How's it going, J?' asked Winston coldly, watching him.

'Not bad, I've done nearly half a

box,' replied J proudly.

'When you've finished that box, you'll only have another eighteen to go. Well done, J,' observed Winston sarcastically.

'I don't see you helping,' shot back J.

'No that's right, you don't,' said Winston, taking another spoonful of fruit from the open tin can he was holding.

'Anyway, I agree with Charles,' said J, picking up the note he'd just ironed and finding it too hot to hold.

'Look, he set us up. That means he put money into us, which means he expects money out of us. You don't need to be an economist to work that out,' said Winston.

'He might think we smoke a lot and burn a bit of profit, but he can't have any idea about the hard currency we've accumulated. I don't know how much it is, do you? We can just slice a bit off the top,' suggested J.

Winston shook his head. He was becoming rather alarmed by all the recent talk of ripping off their employer by stashing away some of their profits on the sly.

'You've got to realise who this chap

we're working for is,' insisted Winston.
'He might look a bit silly, but he's a
fucking lunatic. If he gets the slightest
inkling that we're not throwing straight
dice, then we're going to find out what
the sharp side of a kebab knife feels like.'

Winston was not one to ever refuse
easy money, but he knew that this
particular stash of cash could come with a
death sentence attached to it.

'I still say he won't know,' said J, as he
wandered away from the ironing board
towards the television set that Charles was
watching.

As Winston followed, the heat of the
abandoned iron ignited one of the fifty
pound notes still sitting on the board.
The flames quickly advanced towards the
pile of money at the end of the board.
And these are the guys that want to play
fast and loose with the most mother-
fucking gangster in London, thought
Winston, quickly suppressing the fire.

Winston joined J and Willy sitting on
the sofa in front of the television where
they were glued to a truly terrible daytime
quiz programme. On the sofa opposite
them was Charles and the motionless form

of Gloria, whose flowery dress and top blended perfectly with the cushions and cover of the furniture.

'Why do we watch this shit every afternoon?' said Winston.

'She's going to win the car,' said Willy transfixed.

There was a buzz from the front door and Willy reached behind him to pick up the entry phone that was connected to the entrance intercom.

'Use the cage, that's what it's there for,' said Winston.

'Who is it?' asked Willy into the phone.

'It's Plank. Open up, I want some stuff,' came Plank's voice.

Willy pressed a button on the intercom and the door downstairs opened with a loud buzz.

'This weed is getting quite a reputation, fellas,' said Plank, coming upstairs.

Plank had always been disliked by everyone who met him since he had been a small child. One of the unpleasant results of this was that he had a tendency to appear over friendly, and always smiling at people, hoping to grovel his way into their affections. Winston found him particularly unbearable.

Plank went to sit down on the sofa opposite Winston, and at the last moment realised that he was about to sit on the camouflaged Gloria.

'Jesus! Never saw you there. Hello, love. Enjoying yourself?' There was no answer from the girl. 'Is she er, compos?' Plank asked Winston.

'What do you think?' replied Winston, without bothering to look up.

Plank leaned down for a closer inspection.

'Boo!' said the girl, suddenly coming to life.

Plank stumbled backwards, knocking over a stack of shoe boxes which crashed to the floor, exploding with fifty pound notes.

'Fuck me!' he exclaimed, genuinely surprised and impressed.

'For God's sake,' said Charles, directing his remark at Willy.

'Clean that up, Charles,' said Willy, trying to stand up for himself.

'Sod you, you clean it up,' ordered

Charles.

'Sorry fellas, but that stupid cow scared the fucking life out of me!' explained Plank.

'Never mind, could you please just sit down and stay out of the way?' ordered Winston. 'And look, how much is it you want?'

'I'm after a half weight,' said Plank, trying not to make it obvious that he was watching Charles shovel handfuls of money back into the box. Plank's mind was beginning to have a series of evil thoughts and they were all to do with that money.

'Then that'll be fifteen hundred pounds,' announced Winston.

Willy passed him the scales, and J handed over a bag of goods.

'Any chance of actually seeing your money?' growled Winston.

'Sure, no problem,' said Plank, still keeping one eye on the money on the floor. 'No problem.'

For Eddy, the next two days were an unpleasant and painful blur. He had taken his defeat very badly. All four lads had the

gut-wrenching thought of Hatchet Harry
defingering them one digit at a time, but
Eddy took his failure in the card game
very personally indeed. Knowing nothing
of Harry's dirty tricks, Eddy blamed
himself completely.

Eddy kept away from Soap, Tom and
even Bacon. Reports of him being
spotted wandering around the streets with
a bottle of scotch poking out of his coat
pocket filtered back to the increasingly
worried trio. On one occasion, Eddy was
spotted by a regular of JD's hanging
around the entrance of the bar, but he
hadn't gone inside. He hadn't shaved,
washed, eaten or slept since the disaster
had happened.

On the third day, Soap, Tom and
Bacon met once more in JD's bar and
huddled together in a booth at the back.
Bacon had arrived carrying a copy of *The
Racing Times*, with the name of a
horse ringed.

'The odds are one hundred to one, so
all we need is five grand,' explained
Bacon, as if the race result was a
foregone conclusion.

Soap wasn't keen. 'I'd rather put my

money on a three-legged rocking horse. The odds are a hundred to one for a good reason, Bacon — it won't win. So where is Ed with all the bright ideas?'

'At the bottom of a bottle and has been for two days; it's hit him hard,' replied Bacon.

'It's hit us all hard!' retorted Soap.

'Yeah, but the way things are looking Eddy has got to tell his dad that he is about to lose his bar.'

Tom, who had been pacing the floor in front the other two, suddenly bounded towards them.

'Listen to this one then.' He had another money-making idea.

'I hope this is better than the last one,' interjected Soap.

'You open a company called the Arse Tickler's Faggot Fan Club,' began Tom.

'You what?'

'Then you take an advert in the back page of some gay mag, advertising the latest in arse-intruding dildos, sell it with, er, ... I dunno — "Does what no other dildo can do until now, greatest and latest in sexual technology. Guaranteed results or your money back." All that bollocks.'

Soap and Bacon were listening open mouthed.

'These dils cost twenty-five quid a pop, a snip for all the pleasure they are going to give the recipients. They send a cheque to the company name, nothing offensive, er, Bobbie's Bits or something, for twenty-five. You put these in the bank for two weeks and let them clear.'

Tom paused, and leant forward confidentially. 'Now, this is the smart bit. Then you send back the cheques for twenty-five pounds from the real company name, Arse Tickler's Faggot Fan Club, saying sorry, we couldn't get the supplies from America, they've sold out. How many of those people cash those cheques? Not a single soul, because who wants his bank manager to know that he tickles arses when he's not paying in cheques?' finished Tom.

Bacon rolled the idea over in his mind. It wasn't as stupid as it sounded. 'How long d'you have to wait 'til you see a return?'

'Probably no longer than four weeks,' answered Tom.

'A month? So what fucking good is

that, if we need the money in six — no, five days?' exploded Bacon.

'Well it's still a good idea,' said Tom, defensively. 'If you're so fucking clever why don't you come up with a suggestion?'

'I'm thinking,' said Bacon. 'I am thinking.'

Sitting opposite Dog in their home, Plank was also trying to sell an idea involving money. Dog was sitting at his desk cutting some fine white powder into even finer white powder, while Plank was outlining his idea for their next job.

'So you know these geezers well?' asked Dog. For once he seemed interested in what Plank had to say.

'Well enough. I've been buying gear off them for a couple of years,' replied Plank.

'So what they like, then?'

'Poofs. Nothing at all heavy. Four public school boys. All soft as shite,' he informed Dog.

At that very moment outside the house next door, Eddy was fumbling with his door keys trying to get them into the lock. He finally succeeded and walked slowly indoors, still in his zombie-like state.

Eddy took off his jacket, opened the hall cupboard, and made a half-hearted attempt to hang it up. When the jacket fell off the hanger on to the floor, Eddy collapsed and joined it.

The cupboard doors were wide open and Eddy could hear voices coming through the wall.

'They ponce around in funny hippie clothes all day, talking bollocks. They're just good at growing weed, that's all, and business has got bigger than what they can keep up with,' came Plank's high-pitched voice.

'Listen, they can't be all that stupid if they've got a container load of cash sitting in shoe boxes, a skip-load of Class A gear and you don't think there is anybody sensible involved,' said the much deeper voice of Dog.

At the words 'load of cash', Eddy's attention suddenly perked up.

'What about security?' asked Dog.

'There's one steel gate as you go in, but they never lock it,' reported Plank.

'What do you mean, never? Well, what have they got it for then?'

'I must have been there fifty times and it's never been locked,' assured Plank. 'They're not suspicious. Everybody who goes there are toffs. They're all into that karma crap: "If I don't harm nobody, nobody harms me" stuff.'

In the hall next door, Eddy strained to hear every word.

'And there's no way they can get back to you?' quizzed Dog.

'Even if they could, they'd be too shit scared. I'm a geezer. They've got no muscle, they're gutless faggots,' Plank assured him. 'All we have to do is march in, grab their money and gear, and it's ours.'

With new strength, Eddy got up and walked quickly to the kitchen. He took out his mobile phone and dialled Bacon's number.

'Yeah?'

'Hang on a minute, lads,' said Eddy, with a grin. 'I've got a great idea.'

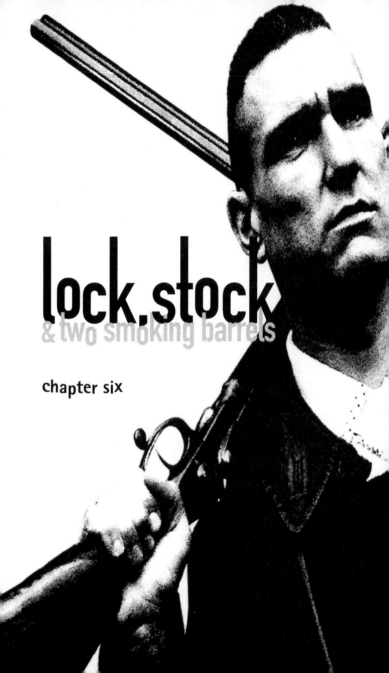

# lock.stock
## & two smoking barrels

chapter six

HATCHET HARRY SAT behind his desk carefully polishing a large shotgun. Opposite Harry, in his normal place on the leather sofa, was Barry the Baptist.

'You sure Big Chris is on his way?' asked Harry as he finished cleaning the weapon. It was one of the many in the collection stored in the cabinet at the rear of his office.

'Should be here any minute,' said Barry, checking his watch. 'I still say you're making a big mistake. That's a lot of money for Chris to be running after. I wouldn't trust him to bring it back here.'

Barry and Big Chris had never been exactly the best of mates, and Harry was used to the constant rivalry.

'What do you know about Chris, eh?' asked Harry, deliberately rattling the bars of Barry's cage. 'You put Big Chris on a job and he makes sure it gets done, no matter what stands in his way. His dad used to collect debts and his dad before that, and that monster of a boy will do the same after he's gone.'

It sometimes seemed to Harry that the Almighty himself had specially assigned the Chris family to collect debts for all eternity. That bunch wouldn't even have qualms about knocking on the door of Old Nick himself, if he was behind with his payments.

Harry trusted Big Chris — not just to get the job done; the old sod actually trusted him. Big Chris had never as much as nicked a nicker in his whole life. He was as straight as an arrow and as strong as the bow that fired it. If he found a lost tenner, Big Chris would search until he found its rightful owner. Harry's only problem was that Big Chris hadn't got the most stable of personalities, and he had a temper like a runaway train.

Heavy footsteps sounded outside Harry's door, heralding Big Chris' imminent arrival and a second or two later the door burst open.

'Hello Harry,' said Big Chris, marching straight into the office. He was inevitably followed by Little Chris, dressed in a near identical dark suit and leather jacket, like a miniature replica of his father.

'Want a drink?' Harry asked Chris.

'Hello son, would you like a lolly?' Barry greeted the smaller version behind.

Little Chris spun round.

'Piss off you nonce!' he spat.

Barry's face cracked into an ugly grin.

'Oi, watch it!' Big Chris warned his son. 'No thanks to the drink, Harry. Me and the boy are all right. Nice shooter,' he added admiring the gleaming gun in Harry's hands.

'Like it? One of a pair, Holland and Holland. Here — you want to hold it?'

'Nah, not my thing thanks, Harry,' responded Big Chris. 'Business good? I imagine that's what I'm here for.'

Harry put the gun down, leaning it against the side of his desk.

'I want you to forget about any other debts at the moment; there are fresher fish to fry!' he announced.

Big Chris never forgot about any debt, ever, but he was already intrigued.

'Go on,' he said.

'It's a bit of a priority. Four young fellas got into a card game a bit deeper than they could handle and now they owe me half a million pounds,' Harry told him proudly.

'How much?' chipped in Little Chris. Even that cynical little bastard was impressed.

'Half a million,' repeated Harry. 'And I want you to get it for me. That, or a certain drinking establishment.'

'I think we'd better sit down,' decided Big Chris. 'Go on, Harry. I'm all ears.'

Three of the four lads on Hatchet Harry's agenda were at that moment making their way to Eddy's house. The phone call earlier had spurred them into intrigued action — particularly as Eddy wasn't spilling the beans until his mates arrived in person.

'Maybe he's won the fucking lottery,' suggested Tom.

'Maybe Harry's died of a heart attack and we're completely in the clear and don't owe anybody anything,' suggested Soap optimistically.

'Maybe I'm the fucking Queen of England,' countered Bacon.

As they approached the house, the lads saw Dog and Plank coming out of the door of the neighbouring hovel.

'Here's trouble,' breathed Bacon to the others.

Dog and Plank looked around the street furtively, then got in their van and drove away.

Bacon got out his keys and opened the front door of the house he shared with Eddy. Eddy was waiting for them in the back room. Three bottles of beer, chilled from the fridge, were ready on the table and the lads took their seats.

'All right, Ed?' nodded Soap.

After the summoning phone call, Eddy had been busy. For the first time since the disaster at the card table he was clean shaven and had changed his clothes. He looked almost human again.

'What's all the flapping about?' asked Tom. 'You told your old man about the bar yet?'

'No, I haven't, because I hope I won't need to,' replied Eddie. 'I've got a plan, so listen.'

No one mentioned the proper mess that the last forty-eight hours had been, or the numerous ideas that Tom, Bacon and Soap had already come up with, each more hopeless and less likely to succeed than the last. Eddy also skipped over his activities of the last two days — although in his case, much of that was due to a complete memory blank.

With new hope in his eyes, Eddy told the others about the conversation he had heard between Dog and Plank through the wall. He described in tasty detail the piles of fifty pound notes lying around in shoe boxes, as well as the piles of drugs. Then he paused and looked around the table as the story sank in.

'Well, what do you want us to do about it?' offered Soap finally.

'Hit the fuckers,' said Eddy, straight.

There was no point mincing words with
this one. He watched this radical idea take
hold.

The silence was deafening.

'I know it sounds a bit heavy, but it's
not like we'll be doing anything illegal,'
he urged.

'I don't know how you reached that
conclusion,' snorted Bacon.

'The bastards next door can hardly
go to the cops and report that they've had
all their drugs and money nicked, can
they?' reasoned Eddy. 'So, no crime gets
reported; so no crime was committed.'

'How heavy are these geezers
anyway?' said Tom.

Eddy shrugged. 'They don't look
all that.'

'Hitler didn't look all that,' chimed in
Soap, who was beginning to think that
everyone else — but Eddy in particular —
had gone slightly insane.

'All right, but for Christ's sake we're
all in the soup and this is the silver spoon,'
said Eddy, a hint of desperation creeping
into this voice for the first time. 'If you
can think of another way to get out of the
shit, let me know. It's not like we've got

all the time in the world either ...'

No one spoke for several long seconds, as the other three rolled over Eddy's idea in their minds. It was a mad, bad, risky and downright fucking dangerous gamble, but it was also the best idea that any of them had come up with so far. It was the best idea by a long chalk.

'I'm game,' said Bacon, suddenly declaring himself up for the job.

'Me too,' agreed Tom.

'Oh, God!' said Soap. He could see where this was going.

It was one thing allowing twenty-five thousand pounds of his money to be used as a stake in an illegal card game, but taking part in an armed robbery was quite another. And worse, he knew that if the other three were in, then so was he. Not that it mattered what he said. There was no way he would ever let them down, but he thought he'd left this sort of thing behind. Now it was happening again. They were pulling him back in by the hairs on his balls and it was making his eyes water.

'We hit them as soon as they come back from the job. We'll be waiting and prepared for them,' promised Eddy. 'They might be a bit armed,' he added, lowering his voice.

'What was that? Armed? What do you mean, a bit armed?' exclaimed Soap. 'Armed with what?'

'Armed with bad breath, colourful language, and a feather duster!' retaliated Eddie. 'What do you think they will be armed with? Guns, you tit!'

Soap kicked back in his chair. 'Guns! You never said anything about guns. A minute ago this was the safest job in the world. Now it's turning into a bad day in Bosnia.'

'Jesus, Soap, stop being such a mincer. I've thought about that and ...'

'And what exactly?' interrupted Soap.

'And we'll just have to find out who's going to be carrying them,' reasoned Eddy.

'Carrying them? They could all be carrying them,' insisted Soap.

'No, only one of them is in charge of them going to the job. So I assume the same one will be carrying them when he comes back from the job,' was Eddy's cool reply.

Soap stood up and began pacing the room.

'Oh, you assume, do you? What do they say about assumption being the brother of all fuck-ups?' he bellowed.

Tom shot him a disparaging glance.

'It's the mother of all fuck-ups, stupid!' he said.

'Well, excuse me. Brother, mother or any other sucker, doesn't make any difference. They are still fucking guns, and they still fire fucking bullets!' shouted Soap, finishing his rant.

It was a well-known fact that Soap always had to register his protest before he went along with things. It seemed that armed robbery was no exception to the rule.

'Soap, if you've got a better idea how to get five hundred thousand pounds in the next few days, then please let us know,' said Eddy calmly. 'In the meantime, Tom, can you talk to Nick the Greek about moving the weed once we've got it?'

Tom nodded.

'We're gonna need some shooters as well,' added Eddy.

Soap collapsed back into his seat in mock protest.

'Jesus!'

Bacon was lost in his own thoughts. Not only was this the best way — probably the only way — out of their problems, but he was rapidly beginning to warm to the idea of robbing those thieving bastards next door. There was a certain Robin Hood quality to Eddy's plan, given the fact that the evil sods they were going rob made their daily bread by doing exactly the same to other people. In fact, it was almost heroic.

Bacon was up for it. Bacon was well up for it, he decided.

As soon as Tom left Bacon and Eddy's place, he called Nick the Greek on his mobile phone.

'How's the diet?' asked Nick.

Tom was in no mood for messing around.

'I need a meet,' he said simply. 'How about the Hope and Glory in ten minutes?'

'How about the Merry Fiddlers?' came Nick's voice through a wave of static.

'That's miles from me. Why that dump?'

'Because I'm sitting in the saloon bar of it right now, and because I've just ordered a pint that I don't intend to waste,' Nick informed him.

Faced with that kind of heavy, intellectual argument, Tom gave in and drove straight over.

By the time he got there, Nick had finished whatever dodgy business he had been doing and was amusing himself by inserting money into a Triple Crown fruit machine in the far corner of the pub.

'All right, Nick?' nodded Tom.

'You want a drink?' asked Nick.

'Yeah, cheers.'

'Great, so do I. The bar's over there,' pointed Nick.

Eager to keep Nick sweet, Tom bit back the usual rebuff went off to get a couple of pints.

'You got any pound coins?' said Nick, slotting yet another one into the machine. 'I'm nearly out.'

'Jesus, Nick! Do I look like a cashpoint machine?'

'No, you look like a fat man who
wants to cut back on his beer,' Nick
grinned.

Tom searched his pockets and found
a single pound coin which he duly handed
over. Then he explained the situation
to Nick.

Obviously, he left out the bit about
how the card game had gone wrong, and
the bit about owing Harry half a million,
and most certainly the bit about the
planned armed robbery. In fact, about the
only thing that Tom did tell Nick was that
he'd soon have a huge quantity of weed to
get shot of.

'Weed?' exclaimed Nick incredulously.
Tom's repertoire was electrical stuff; weed
was another ball game altogether.

'Yeah, but not normal weed,' Tom
assured him. 'This is some fuck-up, skunk
class A, I-can't-think-let-alone-move shit.'

'Doesn't sound very good to me,'
commented Nick.

'No, well me neither, but it depends
on what flicks your switch. The light's on
and burning bright for the masses with
this stuff,' said Tom, watching the Greek's
moves on the fruit machine.

'I nearly had three melons earlier,' tutted Nick, mesmerised by the whirling barrels.

'Anyway, do you know anyone?'insisted Tom.

'Yes, Rory Breaker,' answered Nick immediately, waiting for Tom's predictable reaction.

'Rory Breaker — that fucking madman with an Afro? I don't want anything to do with him.'

'You won't have to. Just get me a sample.'

'No can do,' said Tom.

'What's that?' asked Nick. 'A place near kat-man-doo? Meet me half way, mate.'

'Listen, it's all completely chicken soup,' Tom assured him.

'It's what?'

'It's as kosher as Christmas.'

'The Jews don't celebrate Christmas, Tom,' said Nick, rolling his eyes.

'Yeah, well, never mind that now,' Tom said, taking a quick look around the bar. There were no customers within earshot. 'I also need some artillery. You know, a couple of sawn-off shotguns.'

'Bloody hell, Tom. That's a bit heavy!'

Tom shrugged his shoulders, trying to look as if planning an armed robbery was a once a week event for him. Nick wasn't taken in.

'This is London, not the Lebanon! Who do you think I am?'

'I think you're Nick the Greek,' said Tom, knowing that a little brown-nosing wouldn't go amiss.

The barrels of the fruit machine stopped, revealing a cherry and two oranges with crowns on the top of them.

'You wanna hold those two,' suggested Tom.

Nick pressed the hold buttons and played again using his last pound coin. Another orange with a crown appeared and the machine began churning out pound coins like they were going out of fashion.

'You lucky bastard,' whistled Tom admiringly, then did a double-take. 'That's my fucking money. My pound won that!' he declared.

Nick scooped up his winnings, which nearly filled both pockets on his jacket with about fifty quid in each.

'And never let it be said I forget my friends,' he said, reaching into the left hand pocket and producing a single pound coin. 'Here's the quid you lent me.'

'Bastard.'

'But it's not all bad news,' smiled Nick, 'I'm seeing Rory later on this afternoon anyway, so I'll talk to him about your weed surplus then. Okay?'

'What've you got happening with Rory Breaker then?' asked Tom.

'I bought a stereo system dirt cheap; I'm selling it to him for seven hundred quid,' said Nick with a big grin.

Tom was outside and halfway across the car park before he realised which stereo Nick was referring to.

'Bastard!'

Nick the Greek was as good as his word. First he saw a pair of out-of-towners he knew had a pair of guns for sale, then he then paid a visit to the spacious and stylish offices of Rory Breaker to set up the disposal of the weed.

Rory's main office was a cacophony of seventies funk and football souvenirs.

Rory was wearing his usual solid black suit, topped with his trademark huge Afro hairstyle. He always sat behind a large raised desk which went a long way to compensate for his less than tall physical stature. One side of the office was taken up with a wall of televisions stacked one on top of another and connected to a video recorder next to them.

As Nick walked in the televisions were displaying a motor race. They should have been showing a video of one of Rory's favourite football teams, but Rory's helpers had fucked up and brought him a tape of an American Football game instead. Quite sensibly hating American football more than almost anything else in the entire world, Rory had had to fall back on motor racing instead.

At his bidding, two of Rory's helpers unloaded the stereo from the back of Nick's car.

'Sit down, Nicholas,' invited Rory.

Nick took a seat on the low sofa directly in front of Rory's desk. The whole set up was designed to give Rory the advantage at all times. In front of the sofa was a glass topped table — a new addition since Nick's last visit.

'Very nice,' said Nick, indicating the table.

'It is very nice, Nicholas,' agreed Rory.

Another of Rory's helpers thrust a glass of cold orange juice into Nick's hand. Nick nodded a quick 'thank you.'

'So tell me about this weed again,' ordered Rory.

'It's the best, most mind-blowing, sense-numbing, Class A weed you ever had.'

'I've had some very Class A material in my time, Nicholas. Very Class A indeed.'

'This is better than that,' insisted Nick the Greek. 'I can, without hesitation, say that this will be the best stuff you've ever had.'

'I can, without hesitation, say that you'd better be right,' threatened Rory. 'How much does your man want for it?'

Nick hadn't got as far as thinking about the price yet.

'My man wants five thousand a key,' he ventured.

'I don't normally have anything to do

with weed, Nick, but if it's what you say it is, I'll give him three and a half thousand a key — that's if it is what you say it is,' nodded Rory. 'I don't want to touch it after a sample. I'll leave you in the capable hands of Nathan here.' He gestured to a huge mountain of a man standing behind Nick.

Then Rory stood up and, leaning over the desk, looked Nick straight in the eyes.

'Nathan will work out the details, but get this straight. If the milk turns out to be sour, I ain't the kind of pussy who will drink it. Know what I mean?' said Rory.

Nick knew exactly what Rory meant. He also knew it was time to leave. He reached forward to put his glass down on the table and caught Rory's suddenly alarmed expression in the corner of his vision.

The entire glass table top shattered with a huge crash.

Nick made a very swift exit and didn't look back.

'Jesus! It looks like a bomb site,'

exclaimed Dean, bringing the car to a halt in the middle of a derelict area. All around were the broken walls of homes long since abandoned.

'This is where he said to meet him, Gary. Under the arches, by the garage he said.'

Dean's passenger didn't respond. Gary and his hair were still very much suffering from the unexpected shotgun blast during their raid on the Appleton Smythe's manor. Dean had done his best to help Gary hide the damage, but it still didn't look anything near normal.

'You all right there, Gary? If you don't feel like doing the talking, I'll do the talking today, okay?' offered Dean.

Gary made no attempt to speak, but he began to fumble with the car door handle with his left hand.

'Do you want to get out there, Gary? Let me help you, mate,' said Dean, racing around to the other side of the car. He helped Gary out of the door and to his feet. 'Don't you go wandering off again, okay. Stay near the car.'

Dean checked the surroundings to make sure they were alone, then opened

up the car's boot. Inside were the
shotguns that had been in Lord Appleton
Smythe's gun cabinet. Dean had taken
them all, just as Barry the Baptist
had ordered.

On top of the guns were stashed
several other little goodies. Dean had
already started selling them off to anyone
who'd give him cash.

Moments later, Barry the Baptist
appeared, heading towards them across the
rubble. As he got nearer he caught sight of
Gary.

'Is your hair supposed to look like
that?' he commented. 'All right, small
stuff?' he offered Dean.

'Enough of the small stuff,' said
Dean. 'Next time we do a job like that
we're going to want more money, or we're
going back to post offices and cars.'

'Where are the guns?' asked Barry,
ignoring the inference.

'In the boot,' Dean told him,
stepping out of the way so that Barry
could see directly inside the large luggage
compartment. He cast his eyes over the
fourteen long rifles of varying ages and
value. He could see no sign of the

hammer-lock guns that Harry had pointed out to him in the Christies catalogue.

'Where are the others?' demanded Barry.

'There weren't no others,' said Dean.

Barry had a short fuse at the best of times, but it was rapidly becoming non-existent. Who did these fucking Scousers think they were?

'Stop fucking around. Where are the others, the old ones?' he yelled.

'I don't know what you mean,' Dean, genuinely confused.

'There were two old hammer-lock guns. Where are they?' said Barry seriously.

Inside Dean's brain something was finally stirring.

'Not in the gun cabinet there wasn't. These, here, are everything from that cabinet,' Dean told him. 'But there was a couple of old hammer-lock muskets the butler was carrying.'

'Those are the guns I fucking want,' said Barry with a patronising smile.

'But those weren't in the cabinet, and you said anything not in the cabinet was ours,' complained Dean. 'I sold them, about an hour ago.'

'Well, you had just better un-sell them, and sharpish,' ordered Barry.

'We had to sell them! We needed the money and ...'

'I am not fucking interested,' spelled out Barry, calmly interrupting him.

Then he turned the volume up and began shouting, wildly poking the air with his forefinger, while his face contorted into a ugly mass of angry flesh.

'If you don't want to end up counting the fingers that you haven't got, I suggest that you get those guns back, quick!' he finished.

After what seemed like a lifetime, Dean and Gary watched Barry depart across the wasteland, back the way he had come.

'Fucking hell, Gary, he's really pissed off,' groaned Dean. 'We'd better make a call and get those guns back, or we're fucking right in the shit. I just hope our man hasn't fucking sold them already.'

His partner made no response. Gary stared into the middle distance, watching a bird flying across the sky.

Sighing gently, Dean guided Gary

gently back into the car and buckled his safety belt. Then, he climbed into the driver's seat and started the engine, putting the car into reverse.

What Dean didn't know was that it was already much too late. Across town, about a mile to the east, the guns in question had just changed hands for the second time that day.

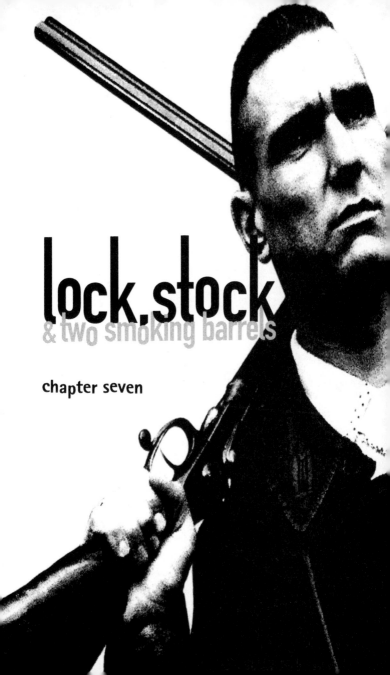

# lock.stock
## & two smoking barrels

chapter seven

SOME NINETY MINUTES before Barry had told Dean and Gary to get the hammer-lock guns back, the items in question were already being sold on.

Earlier that evening, Tom had opened the sliding metal doors that protected his lock-up to find himself looking directly at the backside of Nick the Greek. Nick's wide and bulbous arse was not a pretty sight at the best of times, let alone when you were in the middle of planning your first armed robbery.

Nick lifted an item out of the side door of his small red van and lit himself a cigarette, taking a deep drag. He walked purposefully into Tom's lock-up and unwrapped the bundle in his arms, revealing the two ancient hammer-lock guns.

'Jesus, if I pick them up will they stay in one piece?' asked Tom. 'Where did you get those from?'

'I got contacts,' stated Nick slyly.

Nick could see Tom was rather surprised at the age of the equipment on offer and that a lot of reassurance, not to mention huge quantities of bullshit, would be required to complete this little transaction.

'Listen, Tom, I know they're old, but if you pointed them at me, I'd shit myself or do whatever you told me. Either way you still get the desired effect.'

Tom picked up one of the guns for a closer inspection and ran his palm along the length of the barrel.

'They look nice, I agree ... but lacking in criminal credibility just a bit, aren't they? I might get laughed at.'

'No one will laugh at you, Tom,' said Nick, stony-faced.

'How much do you want for

these muskets?'

'Seven hundred each.'

'What's that — a pound for every year they've been about? I know they're antiques, but I ain't paying antique prices,' insisted Tom, taking a pretend shot at the end wall. 'They're a bit long, aren't they?'

Nick shook his head; clearly Tom had no idea about this year's gun fashions.

'Sawn-offs are out, Tom. People like to have a bit more range now days.'

'Range?' grunted Tom. 'I don't want to blow the arse out of the country, granted, but I don't want anybody blowing a raspberry at me either. I want to look fucking mean.'

'Of course you'll look mean,' said Nick, hiding his smile. 'You'll look really scary.'

Tom put the gun back down with its twin.

'All right, let's forget about them for the time being. What about your geezer that sells drugs?'

'Rory Breaker is ready and standing by. You get the stuff to me, I'll pass it on, okay?' Nick informed him.

'I'll need to get rid of it fast.'

'You will. And you stand to make a lot of money out of this, Tubby Tommy,' predicted Nick.

Tom and Nick began to discuss the price of the guns. As with all their deals, it was a discussion which would go on for some time.

'JD — there's someone here to see you.'

Alan the Barman stuck his head through the entrance to the private back room of JD's bar where his boss was going over some figures. From the look on Alan's face, JD could tell that this visitor wasn't someone he wanted to see.

'Who is it?'

'You'd better come,' said Alan, disappearing back to the main bar.

JD sneaked a peek around the corner of his door. Leaning on the bar, large as life and twice as ugly, was Big Chris, right-hand man and debt collector extraordinaire for Hatchet Harry. JD's mind went into overdrive.

In the few seconds it took him to walk over, JD pieced together the few whispers he'd been hearing about Eddy, Harry and a game of cards. Eddy obviously owed Harry money. Probably big money — maybe a hundred thousand or so. Fucking idiot.

'Evening, Chris. Can I get you a drink?' asked JD, adopting his best customer-friendly face.

'No, thank you, JD, I'm all right at the moment,' was the reply.

'I hope this is a social call, Chris?' said JD, knowing full well that it wasn't.

'Well, not exactly,' answered Chris honestly. 'See, I'm here about your son. It seems he's in the unfortunate position of owing my employer a considerable sum of money.'

'Well, he's not here. In fact I haven't seen him all day,' JD told him.

'It wasn't him that I've come to see, but you,' said Big Chris. 'Your boy Eddy owes Harry half a million pounds.'

Half a million pounds — fucking, fucking idiot, thought JD. How many times had he warned Eddy about playing cards with Harry? But he wasn't about to let Big Chris see his shock and returned the man's gaze with complete cool and an unconcerned expression.

'Harry is looking to get his money

back a bit sharpish, and Eddy has three days left to come up with the goods,' continued Big Chris. 'Since I am in charge of making sure this debt gets paid — and you know how much I hate unpaid debts — all this puts me in a difficult position.'

'What's it got to do with me?' asked JD blankly.

Big Chris decided that JD clearly wasn't grasping the full seriousness of the imminent threat to his only son and heir.

'I understand this must've come as something of a shock, but I'll tell you how this can be resolved by you, the good father,' he explained.

'Go on.'

'Harry likes your bar. He likes it very much,' said Big Chris, looking around.

'That's nice.'

'Harry wants your bar.'

'So?'

'Do you want me to draw you a picture?' asked Big Chris, growing impatient.

'Look, that boy of mine doesn't know his arsehole from his earhole, or you from a hoodwink,' insisted JD firmly. 'This bar is mine. It's got nothing to do with him.'

'What, and I care? Remember, you do have the luxurious advantage of being able to sustain your son's life,' threatened Big Chris.

JD leaned forward and adopted a much softer tone of voice.

'And you do have a reputation, so I'll choose my words very carefully.' JD paused. He wanted to get the wording of his message to Harry exactly right. 'Tell Harry to go fuck himself.'

Big Chris smiled at how close JD was sailing to the wind just to make his point.

'I'll put that down to shock, but only once. Only once can or will I let you get away with that,' the debt collector told him. 'Your son's got three days to find half a million quid. So make up your mind which you prefer: your bar or your son.'

With business over for now, Big Chris walked out of the bar to where Little Chris was waiting in their car.

Just wait until I see Eddy, thought JD as he watched the big man leave.

'There's nothing to worry about, it's going to be easy,' came Plank's voice through the wall, completely unaware that he was playing to an avid audience. His voice passed into an amplifier, through a digital sound scanner and was then recorded on a huge reel-to-reel tape machine.

Sitting by this huge pile of recording equipment was Bacon, wearing a pair of black headphones. He checked that the recording levels were set correctly, then gave Eddy a big thumbs up sign.

Eddy had recently returned home to find that during his absence the kitchen had been converted into what amounted to a high-tech surveillance studio. Bacon had obtained all this new spying equipment on extended loan from another dodgy contact known as Nigel the Nose. It was evident that he was enjoying himself immensely.

'There's no such thing as easy in my experience,' came Dog's voice next door. 'And, if you think this is going to be easy, you're a dick. It may be easier than most, but it's not going to be easy.'

Dog had called a meeting of the whole gang to discuss their next job.

Plank, Paul, Mick and John knew only
too well that 'discuss' meant 'tell'.

On the other side of the wall, Eddy
and Bacon listened intently to every word,
while the tape machine recorded them for
future playback.

'We're using your van, Paul, okay?
We'll need something about that size cos
we'll have money and the weed,' said Dog.

'How're we getting in? Kick the shit
out of the door as usual?' asked Paul.

'No, this place is up some stairs so
we'd stick out like the balls on a bulldog,'
replied Dog. 'Plank's going to get us in,
aren't you?'

'Yeah,' nodded Plank, pleased to be at
the centre of things for once. 'I'm going
up first. They know me, so those poofs
will open the door straight away, no
messing.'

'What about security?' piped up
Mick.

'There's a cage, but it's never locked,
is it Plank?'

'No.'

'And it better bloody not be locked
tomorrow,' warned Dog. 'Once Plank is
in, he'll get the rest of us in. Then we get

nasty with a couple of them. Shit them up, scare them, then gag 'em.'

At the mention of getting nasty, Mick's face broke into a broad smile. Getting nasty was one of the things Mick did best and he liked to be creative about it.

'I can't see these wankers giving us a problem, but they might have a couple of tools hanging around like any cowboy, so we'll watch it,' continued Dog. 'When the job is done, we'll come straight back here, unload, and Robert's your father's brother. Everybody savvy?'

'Sweet,' came the unanimous response.

'Right, tomorrow morning, eight o'clock we'll do it. Apparently these slags don't get out of bed until midday. Lowest ebb and all that, and that's just how I like it,' finished Dog.

Next door, Eddy and Bacon heard the meeting break up and looked at each other with some alarm. This was it.

'Jesus,' exclaimed Bacon.

It was really happening. If Dog was going through with his raid, then that meant they were going through with theirs.

'It's happening tomorrow morning,' said Bacon.

'I know, I did hear. I was listening and that particular titbit of information had not escaped me,' shot back Eddy as a touch of nerves kicked in.

'Jesus,' repeated Bacon.

'Look, I've got to go and meet Soap. He's getting some stuff,' said Eddy, getting to his feet. 'I'll tell him we're on for tomorrow and see you back here later with the fat man, okay?'

'What's this stuff he's getting then?'

'I don't know. Stuff for the job is all he said. If I don't get down to JD's quick we may never find out,' said Eddy making a break for the door.

About twenty minutes later Soap unveiled his 'stuff for the job'. It looked suspiciously like four balls of black wool.

'What do we do with these — throw them at the enemy?' said Eddy.

'No, you put it on your head, stupid,' said Soap. He unrolled one of the balls to reveal a black balaclava helmet which he slipped over his head. There were holes for Soap's eyes and mouth; otherwise his features were completely hidden. 'See?

What your well-dressed urban terrorist is wearing this year.'

Eddy was not impressed. 'Christ! Take that off!'

'Listen, if you think I'm going to turn up clean-shaven with a grin on my face, you've got another think coming,' Soap told him. 'These fellas that we're doing over — correct me if I'm wrong, but they are your next door neighbours, right?'

As soon as the words had left Soap's mouth, Eddy realised that Soap might actually have a point.

'Seeing as how they live next door to you and Bacon, I thought it might be a good idea if we disguised ourselves just a little bit,' continued Soap, seeing the change in Eddy's expression.

Eddy decided that, in fact, Soap had a very good point indeed. Possibly a life saving point.

'Right, err ... good thinking, Soap,' he said, backing down quickly.

Flushed with his early success, Soap revealed the second part of his surprise.

'But that's not all, I brought weapons as well,'

'Weapons? What do you mean, weapons?' asked Eddy incredulously.

'These.'

Soap reached under his jacket and produced a rolled-up piece of green canvas. He unfurled it, revealing a stash of six vicious looking knives and flourished them proudly.

'Jesus! Let's keep them covered up, eh?' suggested Eddy, grabbing the bundle from Soap.

He shot a look around JD's bar. No one else seemed to have spotted Soap's deadly cutlery display yet and Eddy wanted to keep it that way. He laid them on the counter in front of him.

'Couldn't you have got anything a bit bigger?' remarked Eddy, sarcasm dripping from every word.

'Like this?' answered Soap, miraculously producing a two-foot-long machete from his trouser leg. 'What do you think?'

Eddy had seen enough.

'I think you need help,' he yelped. Spotting Alan at the other end of the bar he called, 'Can we have a couple of drinks, please?'

Alan looked grim as he approached

Eddy, like he had bad news.

'Have you seen your dad?' he quizzed. 'Hatchet sent one of his men around.'

This was bad news all right. This was very bad news indeed.

'Oh shit. When?'

'Last night,' came a familiar voice from behind Eddy.

Eddy spun round. As he turned, Eddy's jaw was greeted by JD's fist. It was a well-timed punch and Eddy went down immediately, hitting the floor hard.

JD adjusted his jacket, nodded at Soap then walked away, unruffled. Soap gawped with shock, almost as if he'd received the blow himself. Then a voice from below jolted him back to his senses.

'Don't help me up, then. I'll just lay here, shall I?'

At Bacon and Eddy's house, final preparations were being made for the job next day. Tom had just arrived with the guns and he raised his eyebrows when he saw Eddy's face.

'Ed — Christ, what happened to your jaw?'

'I walked into somebody's fist, okay?' said Eddy, making it clear that he didn't want to talk about it.

The lads gathered in the back room, stepping over the junk and rubbish that covered most of the floor space. Since doing the deal with Nick the Greek, Tom had grown rather fond of the old muskets and presented them to the gang with a certain amount of pride.

'These are our weapons,' he said, unwrapping the cloth that hid and protected his recent purchases.

There was now less than ten hours to go to the job itself, and the fact that these guns appeared to have been manufactured some time during the Stone Age, rendered the boys speechless.

'Where did you get those from? A fucking museum?' demanded Soap at last.

'Nick the Greek, actually,' said Tom, aiming one of the muskets and pretending to shoot out the light bulb.

'How much did you part with?' asked Bacon, picking one up for a closer look.

'Seven hundred the pair,' Tom told him.

'That's drachmas, I hope. I'd feel safer with a chicken drumstick,' scoffed Soap. 'Those could do more harm than good.'

The others didn't display any more confidence.

'Jesus, Tom, do they even work?' queried Bacon.

'I dunno, but they look nice. I rather like them,' observed Tom. He held one out to Soap so he could admire the fine craftsmanship of the barrel. The gesture wasn't appreciated.

'Oh, that's top of the list of priorities, is it? How nice they look!'

'Ladies, if you don't mind, can we please get back to the more important issues?' said Eddy from across the room where he was reclining on the threadbare sofa. The others stopped bickering and listened.

'We've only got two real guns — apparently that's what they are. So, tomorrow morning we watch the bastards leave,' he outlined. 'We need someone outside to keep watch, sitting in a car down the end of the street. That'll be to warn us when they're back, and to come in after them, last.'

Tom caught Eddy's eye, silently volunteering.

'All right, that's the fat man's job,' agreed Eddy. 'The rest of us'll find a good place to hide next door then, when it sounds like the right time, we jack-in-the-box, look nasty and stuff, and cocoon them in gaffer tape. Then we nick their van, bung the gear into a new van and bring it back here.'

'Tasty,' nodded Bacon, still holding one of the old guns.

'If we're all out of our hiding places quickly, it's the last thing they'll expect,' said Eddy. 'And if Tom, or anyone else for that matter, feels like kicking them around a bit, I'm sure it won't do any harm.'

Tom nodded in agreement.

'A bit of pain never hurt anyone ... er, if you know what I mean,' broke in Soap eagerly. 'Also, I think knives are a good idea. You know, big fuck-off shiny knives — ones that look like they could skin a crocodile.'

Eddy sank back into the sofa as Soap went off on one about his fucking knives again.

'Knives are good,' insisted Soap, 'because they don't make any noise. And the less noise they make, the more likely we are to use them. That'll shit them right up and make us look like pros. Guns for show, knives for a pro,' he finished, with a strange glint in his eyes.

The lads looked at Soap with extreme suspicion. This was a side of the boy they'd never experienced before.

'Soap, is there something about you we should know?' asked Tom.

'I am not sure what's more worrying — the job or your past,' remarked Bacon.

'Right, let's get some shuteye,' ordered Eddy, wrapping things up. 'Tomorrow we've got work to do.'

Bacon was first up in the morning, keeping watch in case Dog brought the time of the job forward for some reason. He didn't though; if anything, the gang was now running slightly late.

'Where are those bastards?' said Bacon to himself as he waited by the front room window, sneaking a look out of a crack in the curtains.

Finally there was movement as Dog

and his gang appeared from the house.

'Here they are, ladies,' hissed Bacon quietly.

Soap, Tom and Eddy crowded around the window to get a look at their future victims heading off on their own job.

'What the fuck are they wearing?' exclaimed Soap, seeing that each of them were dressed in brown overalls. 'Are they going out to shift a piano? I thought this was meant to be a robbery.'

'Where did they get those outfits from?' wondered Eddy, clocking immediately that perhaps costumes were a very good idea: it hid what clothes the gang were really wearing and make everyone look the same.

'Yeah, not a bad idea that,' Tom and Bacon agreed, catching on.

'I've got some overalls just like that at the lock-up,' offered Tom.

'Nip round and get us some,' ordered Eddy. 'And move it — we don't know how long they're going to be.'

Tom was on his way before Eddy had finished speaking.

At the grass-house, Winston and his

colleagues were blissfully unaware that at that moment disaster — violent, bloody disaster in the form of Dog's gang — was heading straight towards them.

Winston already had more than enough on his mind right now. Today was the day that all the money they had been collecting from their customers for the last few months had to be counted, packaged and shipped out to their backer. Although Winston had woken Willy, Charles and J up at the unfamiliar and ungodly hour of six o'clock to get them started, progress had been sleepy and slow, and they were running well behind.

'Next box please, Willy,' ordered Winston, impatiently. 'Come on, come on.'

'We're going as fast as we can, Winston,' groaned Willy. 'If we count any faster we just lose track and have to start again. Chill, man.'

'I don't feel like chilling,' replied Winston, looking at his companions with barely disguised contempt.

Winston, Willy and Charles were sitting around the low coffee table in the centre of the main area surrounded by boxes of counted and half-counted money. Gloria, as usual, was slumped semi-conscious on the far sofa.

Why did they always have to leave everything until the last minute, Winston wondered. This should have all been finished days ago.

'Move it, you fucking jelly-heads!' he shouted. 'You've been up for two hours — you should have got somewhere by now. The gear and the money have got to be out of here before twelve.'

'It will be,' said Charles. 'Relax.'

'I do not feel like fucking relaxing,' shot back Winston.

A loud buzz from the intercom phone indicated a visitor at the front door. Another fucking interruption.

'Who's that?' snapped Winston, looking across to J who was nearest the intercom phone. 'J — don't you dare open the door without using that cage. I'm serious, and find out who it is first.'

J picked up the phone. 'Hello, can I help you?'

Outside, Plank rubbed his hands together; he wasn't used to being out in the cold this early.

'All right, it's Plank,' he said into the intercom. 'Is Willy there?'

Upstairs, J looked across to where Willy was busy counting piles of fifty pound notes and lied.

'No, I'm afraid he's not. He's out at the moment.'

'Well, perhaps you can help?' said Plank, not one to be put off easily.

'Well, perhaps I can't Plank, if you know what I mean,' responded J, coldly.

This wasn't the answer Plank was expecting and he nervously rubbed his hands together again. Time was dragging on. From his position at the top of the stairs leading from the front door down to the street, Plank could see the van where Dog and the gang were hiding out of sight. They were probably getting impatient. Plank needed to get inside, and quickly.

'Look, do you think you could open this door so I can talk to you without shouting?' pleaded Plank.

'Sorry, Plank, I really don't think I can help you,' said J firmly.

'I think you'll find it is in your interest,' tried Plank.

J wondered what the idiot had in mind. 'Hold on,' he said into the intercom. Then he turned it off and looked across at Willy.

'Look, Willy, it's Plank outside asking for you. He says it's in our interest,' J told him.

'I don't care if it's King fucking Kong — he's not coming in here, not today,' intervened Winston.

Willy thought about the situation for a second and decided that he very much wanted Plank to come inside today — mainly because Winston didn't.

'Hold on — we're in business, are we not?' he said, pointing at the money scattered all over the table. 'And correct me if I am wrong, but that is business?'

'Plank is a walking accident we can well do without,' remarked J, still holding the intercom phone on mute.

'Jesus, he's okay. He knows only to buy weight now, so we're looking at a couple of thousand at least,' offered Willy, hoping to sway Winston with money. 'Just one last time.'

In the van outside, Dog and the others were beginning to wonder what the problem was. They could see Plank still waiting on the steps. Why hadn't the wankers let him in yet?

'What the fuck is going on?' said Dog, frustrated at the delay.

'Do you want me to go and have a look, Dog?' asked Mick.

'Stay still, you silly fucker,' commanded Dog. 'We wait.'

Plank gestured at the van, confirming that they shouldn't move until he was inside. Then he pressed the buzzer again.

Winston realised that Plank definitely wasn't going away. Perhaps the quickest way to get back to money counting was to give him what he wanted and get rid of him.

'Willy, this is the last time,' he decided. 'Right, you and all the money are going in the back room. If he knows you're here, we'll never fucking get rid of him. We have work to do, you know.'

'Come on, I can't wait out here all day,' shouted Plank's voice over the intercom.

Winston swept the money on the table into a box and hurried Willy out of the room. As soon as Willy was out of sight, he gave the order to let Plank in.

'All right, just coming,' said J into the intercom, then he disappeared downstairs to open the door.

Outside Plank gave a thumbs-up sign to the waiting van. They were in business.

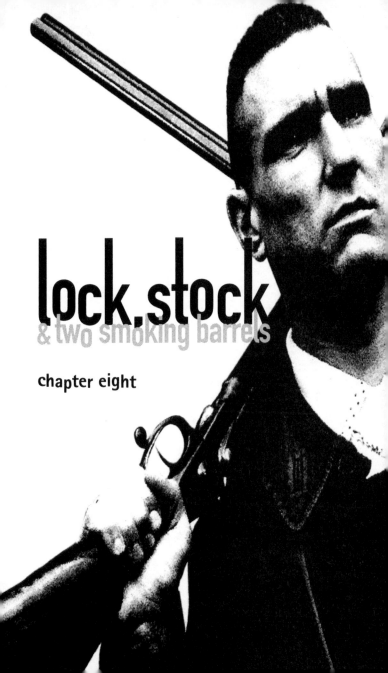

# lock,stock
& two smoking barrels

chapter eight

J WALKED UP TO THE bars of the locked cage and typed in the combination into the digital control that released the outer door. The big oak door that led outside opened and Plank pushed his way through.

'I thought you were going to leave me out there all day,' said Plank, relieved to be inside at last. The thought of explaining to Dog that they weren't going to let him in had been terrifying Plank since the delay had begun.

The first thing that J noticed was Plank's outfit.

'I didn't know you were a removals man, Plank,' he exclaimed.

'What? Oh, yeah, one lives and learns, doesn't one?' said Plank, taking the piss out of J's accent.

Plank started forward, then realised to his horror that a set of thick steel bars blocked his way. The door to the cage was locked, and J was safely on the other side of it with the key.

'Keep the gates locked now, do you?' said Plank, trying to disguise his dismay and wondering what the hell to do.

'Sorry, got to do business like this now; can't be too careful these days,' J observed, taking a drag of the joint he was holding.

Plank decided he had to act immediately and make the little faggot open the cage. If he waited any longer the situation could get a lot worse; J might run upstairs with the key and disappear for good, leaving Plank trapped in the sodding cage.

'I know,' said Plank, changing his tone and grabbing J's collar through the bars of the cage. He slipped out the sawn-off shot gun concealed in his overalls and rammed the end of the barrel against J's right ear.

'Now shut it. You say another fucking word and your right ear goes, another word then your left, okay?' uttered Plank in a low, threatening whisper.

'What are you doing, Plank?' protested J. 'Stop arsing around.'

'What do you think I'm doing? Now unlock the cage,' demanded Plank.

J, who had spent the last few seconds being genuinely confused, suddenly realised what was actually happening and promptly fainted. His body became a dead weight in Plank's grip.

Plank had never seen anyone faint before, and certainly not in the middle of a job.

'Hold on! What are you fucking doing? Oi! I said unlock that fucking cage,' he screamed, as J's body slipped out of his grip and on to the floor just beyond the bars.

As Plank watched incredulously, he saw that J had dropped a large bunch of keys on his slump to the ground and guessed that one of them must open the cage. The keys were just out of arm's reach, so Plank tried using the end of his gun to drag them nearer.

'Fucking hell!' he moaned to himself, knowing full well that Dog would certainly blame him if anything went wrong with this job.

Outside in the van, Dog had had enough of waiting and made up his mind.

'That's it! Go! Go! Go!' he yelled. 'Fucking run, you two!'

Closely following their leader, Mick and John dashed out of the back of the van and up the steps to where the oak door still stood open.

Inside the cage, Plank had just managed to scrabble the keys into his grasp. He was looking through them to decide which was most likely to open the metal cage door when Dog burst through the outer door. He slammed into the back of Plank, sending the keys flying out of his hand and back through the bars of the cage.

'Shit!' cried Plank with frustration. 'I just got them!'

Plank knelt down and started using his gun to try and reach the keys again.

Dog pushed against the closed door of the gate and realised what was wrong.

'This fucking cage's locked, you prick!' he snarled.

'Just hold on, I've got the keys,' promised Plank, urgently clawing them back again with the end of his shotgun.

Dog looked down and saw J's body slumped in heap on the floor on the other side of the bars.

'What the fuck did you do to Little Lord Fauntleroy?' he demanded.

'I didn't touch him, he just passed out,' said Plank still fumbling with the keys in panic, trying to identify the right one.

Upstairs in the living area, Winston suddenly froze. He had been listening to the noises from downstairs and didn't like what he was hearing.

'What's going on down there?' he said to the others.

When they heard the sound of several different voices, Winston stood up with a look of utter horror and realisation on his face.

'Charles, get the rifle out. We're being fucked.'

Downstairs, Plank had still not located the correct key, and Dog was growing more and more impatient.

'Get the sodding cage open now, Plank,' he hollered.

'This must be the one,' said Plank. He fumbled desperately, trying to engage key with hole but getting nowhere fast because of the pressure being applied.

Dog decided to take matters into his own hands.

'Hold this,' he said, passing his weapon over to John. 'Now, Plank, give me the keys.'

Plank turned round and the sawn-off shot gun he'd tucked under his arm swung dangerously close to Dog's groin.

'Don't point that at my bollocks,' growled Dog. 'Point it in there. Planks of wood, I'm working with fucking planks of wood,' he complained to the ether.

Behind Dog, standing at the rear of the cage, Mick decided that it was time he got his gun ready for action. He removed the cloth that had been concealing it, revealing a huge Bren gun. It was without doubt the biggest fucking gun that Dog had ever seen in his life.

'What the fuck is that?' he yelped.

Mick didn't hear him because of the ear muffs he was wearing to protect him from the weapon's fearful noise.

'All right?' he said cheerfully, when he saw Dog looking at him.

Dog pulled up an ear muff. 'What the fuck is that?' he repeated, directly into Mick's ear.

'It's my Bren gun,' said Mick simply.

'Don't you think you could have brought something a bit more fucking practical?' said Dog with despair.

Upstairs, Charles had retrieved the rifle from its hiding place under the sofa. Charles loaded it while Winston watched him, mentally willing him to do it quickly.

'There,' announced Charles at last, holding up the weapon.

'Perhaps, on reflection, an air rifle was not the most hard core weapon to choose,' muttered Winston dryly.

Charles, Willy and Winston crept part way down the stairs, to where the banisters offered a view of the whole ground floor.

'Jesus, what have they done to J?' said Willy, catching sight of J's body lying by the bars.

'They look fucking heavy,' said Charles, his voice quivering with fear.

Plank was still fumbling with the collection of keys, putting his hand through the bars to try each one in turn.

'Take a shot at them, Charles,' ordered Winston.

'What?'

'Take a fucking shot at them. They've not opened the cage yet — maybe we can scare them off,' said Winston.

This seemed to make sense to Charles, and he aimed the gun toward the cage.

'Which one shall I shoot?' he asked.

'I don't know — it doesn't fucking matter. Just shoot one of them,' hissed Winston.

'I could take out their leader. That might stop them,' ventured Charles.

'You're not going to take out fucking anyone because you're using an air rifle,' Winston reminded him. 'Now, just pick one and fucking fire!'

Charles took aim and fired. The gun made a disappointing 'pop' sound as the pellet was propelled across the room and hit the bars of the cage.

Believing they were under fire from real bullets, Plank began to panic.

'Don't you move, or I'll kill the fucking lot of ya!' he screamed at the empty room.

'Who are you going to kill, Plank? There's no one fucking there,' barked Dog impatiently.

A second 'pop' sounded from somewhere on the stairwell and a pellet hit Plank in the neck.

'They fucking shot me!' he gurgled weakly. Terror filled his weasel-like face as he momentarily pictured himself dying with half his neck blown away.

'Well, shoot them back,' suggested Dog, totally unimpressed by the small red welt that had appeared on Plank's neck.

Realising that he probably wasn't dying after all, Plank thrust his gun through the bars of the cage and unleashed an angry round of fire. A thick cloud of smoke erupted from Plank's gun, filling the cage and obscuring everyone's view of the room beyond.

'Jesus, Plank, you could have got

smokeless cartridges. I can't see a bloody thing,' complained John.

A distant 'pop' sounded as another pellet was fired, and John clutched his chest.

'Ah, Jesus! Shit, I've been shot!' he shouted.

Dog rolled his eyes.

'I don't fucking believe this. Could everyone stop getting shot?' he fumed. 'John, sit down and patch yourself up, you tart. It's only a fucking air rifle.'

Dog was about to try and get the situation back under control when an deafeningly loud blast of machine gun fire nearly burst his ear drums. Dog, Plank and John hit the floor, covering their eyes and ears as the noise hammered into their bodies.

When the noise finally stopped, Dog raised his face from the dirt to see Mick standing in the middle of the cage, holding his smoking Bren gun and wearing a big smile on his face. It was the last straw.

'What the fuck was that?' demanded Dog, climbing to his feet.

'That was the Bren gun,' grinned

Mick.

Dog was not amused.

'If you use that again, you're a dead man, do you understand me?' he screamed.

'All right, all right,' said Mick, backing away.

'A dead man. No ifs or buts, you're a fucking dead man,' stressed Dog, prodding Mick in the chest with his finger.

Dog decided that he'd had more than enough of all this mincing about and that it was time to get down to some serious unpleasantness.

'Right, fellas,' he shouted, reaching through the bars and lifting one of J's legs up so that his foot rested against one of the bars of the cage. 'Now, have I got your attention? First, I'm going to blow your friend's toes off.'

Dog paused for about a second, then realised that he'd better just do it.

Boom!

Watching from the relative safety of the stairs, Winston, Willy and Charles saw J enveloped in another cloud of smoke from the gunshot. When it cleared, the grisly results of Dog's point blank range were evident to them all.

'Now, if you want me out of here in five minutes flat, open the fucking gate, now!' bellowed Dog.

'Jesus!' exclaimed Willy, nearly shitting himself. 'What are we going to do?'

'They're going to fucking kill us if we open the gate, man,' gibbered Charles, still holding the air rifle.

'Well, J will certainly get it if we don't. That bastard's serious,' said Winston. 'Look what he did to his toes.'

Dog was still waiting for a response.

'I'm losing patience. Hurry up, girls,' he called. 'Right, his leg's going now.

'All right, all fucking right. I'm coming,' Winston yelled back from the stairs. Then he turned and whispered to Willy. 'Listen, he doesn't know you're here, so sort something out, okay?'

Winston walked slowly down the stairs, leaving Willy with a puzzled and terrified look on his face. What the fuck was he supposed to do against a gang of armed nutters?

Winston reached the bottom of the stairs and emerged in full view of Dog and company.

'And all your friends, there's a good lad,' ordered Dog.

Charles appeared behind Winston.

'There's only three of us here,' Winston lied.

Dog wasn't taking any chances and he aimed his gun at J again. 'I don't believe you. I'm going to blow his leg off.'

'I mean it — there's only three of us here,' pleaded Winston.

'Plank?'

'Yeah, one of them's out,' said Plank concurred, still rubbing his neck.

Dog threw the bunch of keys through the bars of the cage to Winston.

'Open the cage,' he commanded.

The young man moved forward at the speed of an elderly invalid. This was a big mistake, but what else could they do?

Winston unlocked the cage door and Dog stepped triumphantly through. He looked down at Winston with something close to pity, then shook his head. As Winston opened his mouth to speak, Dog delivered a savage headbutt directly to Winston's forehead. Then he grabbed the young man before he could collapse to the floor.

'Upstairs you!' snarled Dog, pushing the stunned Winston ahead of him.

John grabbed Charles and pushed him up the stairs as well.

At last something was going right, thought Plank.

'Tie them up, John. Plank, you come with me and find the money,' ordered Dog, as they reached the main living area at the top of the stairs.

There was no sign of Willy. Winston realised that he must be hiding in the back somewhere.

'The money's in those shoe boxes, over there,' said Plank, eager to get the raid back on track.

Dog took a box off the top of the pile and opened it. It was empty. He kicked over the whole pile, sending the dozen boxes scattering across the floor.

They were all empty.

'Where?' said Dog, simply, putting the barrel of his gun against the back of Winston's head.

'Out the back,' gulped Winston

breathlessly.

'And the weed?'

'Out the back.'

'Point to it,' ordered Mick.

'With what?' asked Winston, a little surprised by the request, given the fact that his arms and legs were tied.

'Your hand, now!' shouted Mick.

'I can't, I'm tied up,' Winston reminded him.

'Well shake your head or something,' suggested Mick.

Winston did his best to indicate the door.

'All right, Plank. Get Paul out of the van, lively,' said Dog. 'Mick, check out that back room.'

'Yes, Dog,' said Plank, racing away.

Behind the door that led to the back room, Willy waited nervously, tightly gripping a two-foot-long machete with both hands. He hadn't had many potential weapons to choose from, and the machete looked by far the most evil.

When Willy heard Dog telling Mick to go into the back he braced himself. This was, without doubt, the worst day of his life. How could that little fucker Plank do this to him?

As Mick stepped through the door, Willy, eyes screwed tightly shut, flailed recklessly with the machete. The blade hacked straight into Mick's arm, slicing right through the flesh until it hit solid bone.

Mick screamed and looked down at his arm. A reflex muscle action caused his trigger finger to twitch, sending a hail of machine gun bullets flying from barrel of the Bren gun.

The first bullet hit Willy's finger, blowing the digit off his hand. The finger flew into the distance, landing somewhere in the middle of the ganja forest.

Mick staggered away blood pouring from the deep wound in his arm.

'Jesus, fuck! Jesus, fuck!' he howled to himself, going rapidly into shock.

'Knife,' ordered Dog simply, and Plank handed him a huge gleaming foot-long blade.

Dog stepped through into the back room and advanced towards Willy. Catching sight of Dog heading straight for him, the young man stopped screaming and slumped to the floor. The pain of his missing finger was bad, but not as bad as the thought of what was going to happen next.

Willy whimpered pitifully as Dog placed the sharp edge of the blade against his throat.

'Enough!' he whispered.

Willy was instantly silent; he knew he was seconds from a painful and bloody death.

'How are you doing, Mick?' asked Dog, furious about the serious damage done to one of his men.

'How do you think I'm doing?' groaned Mick in agony. 'He's fucking nearly chopped my arm off.'

The blade pushed tighter against Willy's neck, not quite breaking the skin. Then, suddenly, the pressure eased as Dog noticed a table piled high with fifty pound notes, all of them neatly packed and stacked.

'Jesus Christ!' he whistled.

In the main living area, Paul had finally come inside from the van and found Mick wandering around, Bren gun under one arm, blood dripping from the other.

'Gordon Bennett! What's been going on here?' he asked, looking more than a little shocked.

'Have a look at this,' called Dog from the back room.

Paul crossed the living room and stepped into the back room, his eyes greedily scanning the piles of money and the indoor ganja garden.

'You got the bags?' asked Dog. 'Can you get all this lot in the van?'

'There's a lot here, all right. But I can't get the whole of Epping Forest there in my van,' replied Paul.

As far as Dog as concerned, this wasn't the right answer.

'Bollocks to can't. I don't want to hear can't. You get it in even if you have to do two trips,' he ordered.

Paul and Dog began to clear up. They grabbed handful after handful of money and threw it into the four black plastic sacks that Paul had brought with him. When they were full, Paul took them outside to load into the back of the waiting van.

As Paul walked down the steps that led down to the street, he saw that a traffic warden was standing by the front of the van, pencil in hand, noting down the licence plate number.

'You've got a ticket already. If you don't move this van now, sir, we will move it for you,' warned the warden as Paul approached.

'I'll only be a minute,' said Paul, putting on a friendly smile and hoping against hope that the warden would let him off.

'You've already been here fifteen minutes,' said the warden, looking at his watch to check the time.

Paul realised immediately that persuasion was futile and that there was only one possible course of action for him to take. He took a quick shifty up and down the street to make sure that the coast was clear.

'Have a look at what's in the back,' Paul offered the traffic warden.

'What?'

'Go on — look,' nodded Paul.

The warden walked down the side of the van towards the rear doors.

'My van's half full,' added Paul encouragingly, as if this meant anything at all.

'So?'

The warden opened the rear doors and peering inside at the collection of black sacks.

'This really doesn't change anything, sir,' remarked the warden firmly.

'I've just got to put you in the back as well, and I'm off,' grinned Paul.

'What ...?'

Paul smacked the traffic warden across the side of the head, and the momentum carried the man's body into the van. Paul checked around the street once more to make sure no one was watching, then lifted up the warden's legs, swung them over and pushed his whole body in.

Back in the upstairs sitting room, Dog was supervising the packing of the last of the money and drugs.

'Plank, do you think that you could manage more than one bag this trip?' he snarled.

'I can't, Dog, it's my neck,' begged Plank.

Dog turned to Mick, who was still nursing his wounded arm.

'How about you?  You dead yet?'

'I'll be fine when I've dealt with that lanky prick,' growled Mick, putting down his Bren gun on the table by the sofa and picking up the machete that Willy had attacked him with.

Mick advanced toward Willy, who was still slumped on the floor, waiting for death.

'Do it quietly,' ordered Dog.

On the nearby sofa, a pair of bright eyes suddenly snapped open.  The eyes zoomed in on the bloodstained figure of Mick walking slowly but purposefully towards Willy cowering in on the floor.  It was Gloria.

She had spent the entire raid comatose and camouflaged on the sofa, unnoticed by Dog's gang.  Gloria had been too spaced-out to be woken up even by the Bren gun.  Until now.

Suddenly alert, Gloria leapt up and lifted the Bren gun from the table in front of her.  She pointed the huge barrel at Mick and pulled the trigger.

Bullets exploded from the machine gun, ripping into Mick's already damaged body.  Huge chunks of flesh exploded all over the room as the bullets transformed him into little more than dog meat.

The impact pummelled the remains of Mick's torso back across the room, shredding his skin and shattering his bones into a million fragments. A foot-long flame blasted from the Bren gun's barrel, and with every bullet fired, a huge metal cartridge was ejected and fell to the floor.

Dog and John dived for cover as the bullets smashed into the room indiscriminately. Plank threw himself behind the television set, seconds before it was hit and exploded.

Winston, Charles and Willy closed their eyes and hoped for the best. This was a side of Gloria they had never seen before. She had found a gear that nobody, not even herself, knew existed.

The gun continued to wreak its devastation around the room until, at last, it spat out its last cartridge and fell silent. Gloria kept her finger pressed tightly on the trigger, unsure what to do next.

Realising the danger had passed, Dog stood up and delivered a well aimed punch to Gloria's jaw, knocking her out.

'Where the fuck did she come from?'

he said, stunned. 'Right, that's fucking it,' he decided, surveying Mick's pulped remains. 'Tie her up — we're getting out of here.'

Leaving Mick's mashed corpse behind, Dog and the gang climbed into the now loaded van and drove away.

'Fucking easy, you said,' growled Dog, scowling at Plank.

'I got shot not you,' responded Plank rubbing his neck again.

Dog turned round and looked at the rear of the van which was stacked high with bags of money and grass. To his further astonishment and disbelief, a head lifted itself into view from among the black sacks.

'You won't get away with this,' babbled the half-conscious traffic warden.

'Paul, what's that?' asked Dog.

'That's a traffic warden,' said Paul helpfully.

'I can see it's a fucking traffic warden,' said Dog. 'But what's he doing in our van?'

'He was going to call the cozzers,' answered Paul, making a left turn and pulling out on to the main road which was thick with early morning traffic.

John reached back, administering a swift right hook to the warden's jaw rendering the man unconscious again.

'Fair enough,' nodded Dog. 'We'll deal with him later.'

Dog and his gang were fifteen, perhaps twenty minutes' drive away from the safety and seclusion of their house. Nothing more could go wrong for them today.

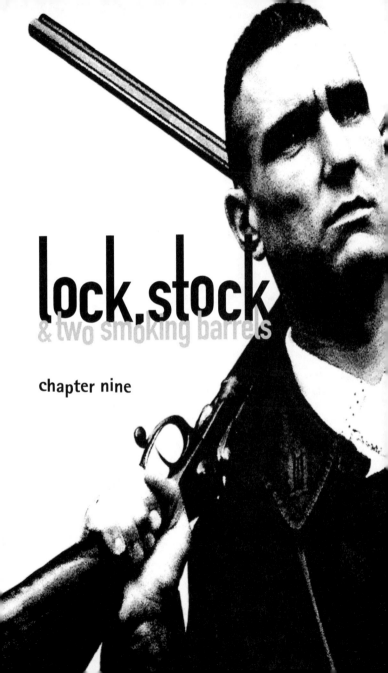

# lock.stock
## & two smoking barrels

chapter nine

AFTER DOG AND HIS GANG had departed
for the raid, Tom had raced to his lock-up
and returned with the promised overalls
for Eddy and the boys.

'It doesn't matter,' assured Eddy,
when Soap complained that the arms in
his weren't quite long enough. 'This is
not a fucking fashion show. Just put it on,
all right?'

The four lads put the overalls on over
the dark clothes they'd selected especially
for the occasion, and pulled their
balaclavas down over their faces.

'We are ready,' announced Bacon, 'to

kick the shit out of anyone.'

'All right, it's like we discussed,' recapped Eddy. 'Tom, you're out the front in the car. When those bastards come back, give us a ring on the mobile. Wait until the last one walks inside, follow him in and get him down on the floor with the rest, sharpish, okay?'

'What about the minicabs?' asked Soap.

'We're not going to do over the fucking minicabs, are we?' snapped Tom.

'No, but we don't want those drivers knowing what's going down, do we?' argued Soap.

On the other side of Eddy's place was a twenty-four hour minicab firm called Speed Cabs — so named because that was what their drivers were on most of the time, was the local consensus. There were always drivers hanging around outside on the pavement waiting for their next unfortunate customer.

Eddy weighed up the chances of them noticing anything and decided that Soap was right. It wasn't worth the risk.

'All right, Tom, if there are drivers hanging around the doorway then ring up and get rid of them, okay?' said Eddy.

'And how the fuck do I do that?'

'Airports,' suggested Soap. 'Cab drivers love airport jobs because they can always fuck you over on the fare. Tell them your whole family's just touching down at Heathrow.'

Tom left the house and returned to his car to keep watch for the gang's return.

Eddy, Bacon and Soap headed out the back into Eddy's postage-stamp-sized garden.

'Bunk us up over the wall,' said Bacon.

Using Eddy's hands as a step, Bacon lifted himself over the wall and dropped into Dog's back garden. He had the sudden awful thought that perhaps one of the gang had stayed behind at the house, but peering through the windows he saw the place was empty.

On the other side of the wall, Bacon could hear Soap and Eddy arguing about who was going over next.

'Ladies, just climb the fucking wall,' hissed Bacon.

While Eddy and Soap got over the wall, Bacon set to work on Dog's back door with his crow bar. The door was reinforced and made of thick metal, but that didn't stop Bacon. Now that they had actually started the job, Bacon found he was enjoying himself in a strange sort of way.

As the others joined him, Bacon finished forcing the door. The lads looked around once more to make sure they weren't being watched, then stepped inside. Soap closed the door behind them.

Inside, they found themselves in a small kitchen which lead to a larger back room. On the wall was a fifties style oil painting of a brunette, in a cheap, white frame. A metal safe sat snugly against one wall, no doubt containing the rewards of Dog's other recent raids.

Soap reached into his pocket, took out a pair of spotless white gloves and began to carefully put them on.

Eddy took a quick look around. Seeing the kettle in the kitchen, he plugged it in. Bacon and Soap exchanged a confused look.

'What are you doing?' asked Bacon.

'Do you want one?' said Eddy, indicating the kettle in front of him.

'No I fucking don't!' Soap exploded, 'You can't make a cup of tea, Edward.'

'The entire British Empire was built on cups of tea,' insisted Eddy, beginning to brew up.

'And look what happened to that,' cut in Soap.

'Well, if you think I am going to war without one, mate, you're mistaken.'

Bacon, who had been watching Eddy closely, suddenly realised that two rather important pieces of equipment seemed to be missing.

'Going to war with what exactly,' Bacon asked Eddy.

Eddy froze.

'You forgotten those guns, haven't you, you dozy prat,' said Bacon, shaking his head.

Eddy's face became a mask of contrition. He put down the teabag he was holding and left the kitchen in an embarrassed silence.

Outside, Tom was sitting in his car, parked on the opposite side of the road. As Eddy collected the ancient guns from their hiding place in the junk-filled sitting room, he called Tom from his mobile phone.

'How we doing, Tom?' asked Eddy.

'Right as rain. I'm going to take care of the minicabs now. I'll call you when Dog and co are back,' replied Tom.

Outside the seedy office of Speed Cabs, three of its drivers were killing time between jobs. Two of them were sitting on wooden chairs, while the other leaned against the doorway.

Tom dialled the number advertised on their doorway. The phone rang several times before being answered by a male voice halfway through having a drag on a cigarette.

'Yeah?'

'All right, mate? Do you do airports?' asked Tom.

A few moments later, a male figure appeared in the doorway of the cab office, sending all three of the men outside scurrying towards their cars. They set off in a convoy, to pick up fares that didn't exist that wouldn't be arriving on the flight from Rome not landing at 16:45 pm.

With the cabs out of the way, there was nothing more for Tom to do except wait.

Inside Dog's house, Eddy, Bacon and Soap had donned their balaclavas and moved into the front room, making final preparations for the imminent return of Dog's mob. The room was empty except for a desk.

Eddy paced around the room, seemingly searching for something he had lost.

'What's up with you?' demanded Bacon, who was sitting on the desk holding both guns.

'Where the hell are we going to hide?' fretted Eddy.

'Don't complicate things,' advised Bacon, who hadn't got that far in his planning. 'Just hide.'

Just then Eddy's mobile phone went and he grabbed it out of his pocket.

'Yeah?'

'We're on,' said Tom's voice, then the line went dead.

The lads heard Dog's van pull up outside and ducked into hurried hiding places. Throwing one of the guns to Eddy, Bacon hid himself behind Dog's desk. Soap squeezed behind a wardrobe on the far wall and Eddy stepped out of sight into the hallway.

Outside in the street, Tom watched the van pull up and began to make his way across the road, pulling his balaclava helmet from his pocket. Dog opened the rear doors of the van and pulled out two black dustbin sacks. He opened the front door to the house and led the others inside.

Dog threw the two sacks on to the floor and sat down at his desk to make a phone call. Plank walked in, still rubbing his sore neck.

'Cor, these weigh a pound or two,' grinned John, throwing his sacks on top of the ones Dog had deposited.

At this, Eddy stepped into view. He pointed the ancient gun straight at Plank, who froze.

'Shut it!' shouted Eddy brutally.

Halfway through dialling the number he wanted, Dog twisted round on his chair and saw Bacon and his shotgun crouching just behind where he was sitting.

'Spin round, big boy,' ordered Bacon, thrusting the barrel towards Dog's head.

Soap burst out of his hiding place, practically launching himself at John, who hurtled backwards on to the wall behind. Soap firmly planted the lengthy blade of his knife at John's throat.

Then the door opened again and Paul collapsed inside, already bowed under a rain of blows from Tom who was just behind him.

'Stay down!' bellowed Tom, as Paul crashed to the floor. Tom slammed the door behind him.

Eddy took a step towards Plank, who was standing stunned by their unexpected appearance. He smashed the handle of his gun up into Plank's forehead. Plank's legs turned to jelly and he hit the ground with a thud.

For Dog, the last few seconds seemed like deja vu in reverse. He couldn't believe that anybody would dare fuck with him like this, let alone in his own home.

'Tie them up, tape them up, face and mouth,' yelled Eddy. Each of the lads produced a roll of brown gaffer tape and set to work.

'Bend over the fucking desk,' Bacon ordered Dog, who still couldn't believe what was happening.

'Keys!  I want keys!' screamed Eddy.

'I'll find you,' promised Dog, coolly.

''Course you will, sweetheart,' replied Bacon.

'I'll find you,' Dog repeated.

'What do you think this is — hide and seek?' asked Bacon, tying Dog's arms behind his back.

'Keys.  I want keys!' ordered Eddy again.

'That one's got them,' said Bacon, nodding towards John who was having his legs secured by Soap.

Soap leant down and quickly felt each of John's pockets.  He soon produced a bunch of keys which he threw to Eddy.

'I'll meet you in the van when you've finished with handsome here,' said Eddy, turning towards the door.  He stepped out into the street and removed his black balaclava in one smooth movement.  Then he checked that the keys worked and started the van.

Soap and Tom brought out the bags that had already been taken inside, while Bacon applied the last of the gaffer tape to their prisoners.

'We're done,' he said, emerging from the building and closing the door after him. He threw the last two black sacks into the back of the van then climbed in himself.

'Drive,' he called to Soap who was sitting behind the steering wheel.

Soap put the van into gear and accelerated.

Bacon checked out of the rear window as they shot off. He half expected that Dog and his gang would come bursting out of the door, shotguns blazing, and give chase, but they didn't.

Looking around him in the rear of the van, Bacon realised that they'd actually done it. They had the weed, they had money and they'd got clean away.

'Well that wasn't so bad, was it?' said Tom, after they'd driven a few blocks in silence.

Soap's expression made it clear that he had a different opinion. 'When the bottle in my arse has contracted, I'll let you know,' he said.

Tom lit two cigarettes and passed one to Soap in the driving seat. Soap grabbed it and took what felt like a long overdue drag.

'Bacon, see what we've got,' suggested Eddy.

'Let's have a butcher's,' said Bacon, turning round and beginning to explore the rear of the van. 'Jesus, there's lots of everything. There's God knows how much of this stinking weed, a shit load of cash and we've got ...' Bacon grabbed what looked like a human head and pulled it from underneath the plastic sacks, '... a traffic warden.'

'What?' yelped Tom, disbelieving his ears.

'A traffic warden. Look at this,' said Bacon, handing over the man's hat as evidence.

As Bacon knelt down to take a closer look, he touched the warden's head with his fingers. Then he examined his fingers, red with fresh blood.

'I think he's still alive. He's got claret coming out of him somewhere,' said Bacon. 'Why the hell would they steal a traffic warden?'

'I dunno, but I don't think we need him,' noted Eddy dryly. 'Knock him out and we'll dump him at the next light.'

'Knock him out? How?'

'Just knock him out,' said Eddy.

'Knock him out with what?' shouted Bacon.

'I don't know. Use your imagination,' shrugged Eddy.

There was the sound of a punch being thrown, then a stifled moan from the back of the van.

'Don't touch him up — knock him out,' complained Tom.

Bacon's face appeared behind Eddy and Tom. His pissed off expression made it clear that he was fed up with being ordered about.

'I'll knock you out in a minute. Look, you want to knock him out, you knock him out.'

'I fucking hate traffic wardens,' said Eddy, meeting Tom's eyes.

Half a second later, Eddy and Tom had both decided that knocking out the traffic warden was an opportunity rather than a problem, and leapt into the back of the van to administer a good kicking.

If Hatchet Harry was honest with himself — and, of course, he was rarely honest with anyone, even himself — he was becoming somewhat concerned.

Eddy and his friends owed him half a million pounds, an amount that they had no hope of finding, yet so far Harry had not heard a peep out of any of them. There were only a couple of days to go before the payment was due in either cash or fingers, and Harry had heard absolutely diddly squat.

By this stage in the proceedings, Harry would normally have expected the grovelling and pleading to have begun. He should have received letters and personal appeals for more time, or part payments. Even Big Chris' visit to JD had produced no reaction from Eddy or the other losers he hung around with. The boys in question had been seen all over the park in the last few days, so he knew that they hadn't done a runner, but what the fuck was going on?

In times of crisis or worry, Harry turned to his friends. Once again he had summoned the impressive figure of Big Chris to his office to give him fresh orders. Harry was at his desk, with Barry the Baptist across the room in his usual position. Between them, dressed in his trademark black, was Big Chris.

'It's about time you gave my young friends a visit, Chris,' said Harry, reclining with his feet up on his antique desk. 'Tomorrow is the day and so far mum's the word. I can't have that now, can I, Baz?'

'No, Harry, you can't,' agreed Barry from the sofa.

'It's a liberty, and I can't have a liberty taken, can I Chris?'

'No, Harry, you can't,' agreed Chris.

Everyone always agreed with Harry.

'It's enough to give me the arsehole. And I can't have the arsehole, can I boys?'

'No Harry, you can't,' agreed Barry and Big Chris in perfect unison.

'Leave it with me, Harry,' added Chris. 'I'll get it sorted.'

Even after two hours bound and gagged in gaffer tape, Dog still couldn't believe what had happened to him. Who would be so stupid as to fuck with them? What kind of pond life could have a brain so small that it thought it could piss around with Dog and live? People were going to suffer for this. People were going to suffer very badly indeed when he caught up with them.

Plank had been the first of the gang to get free, using the sharp edge of one of the legs of Dog's desk to gradually cut through the gaffer tape that bound his hands behind his back.

'The biggest mistake they ever made in their entire fucking lives was leaving me alive!' screamed Dog at the top of his voice as Plank ripped the last of the gaffer tape from his mouth. 'I'm going to fucking kill them.'

'Who'd do a thing like this, Dog?' asked Plank, moving on to Paul and beginning to free him of his sticky bonds. 'I tell you, it's made my neck really hurt.'

'Never mind your fucking neck. I want those walking dead men found and brought here,' ordered Dog.

'They'll be dead when we fucking find them,' added John as his mouth became free of the gaffer tape.

'Dead? They'll be fucking dead, all right. I don't know who they think they are, but I'll find them,' Dog shouted, his face red and sweaty with hatred and fury. 'I don't give a flying fucking fish who they think they are,' he repeated. 'I'll kill — fur and feathers, burning wheel African style, kebab them, peel them, slice them and dice them, hang, draw and fucking quarter them.'

And with that, Dog stomped out of the room, leaving Plank to finish freeing John and Paul.

At that exact moment, the subjects of Dog's extreme tirade were about to finish unloading the contents of Dog's van into a van of their own.

Eddy stood by the rear doors, pulling out sack after sack of weed and money, and throwing them across to Soap, who was tossing them into the back of Tom's van.

'About a dozen more,' Eddy informed him.

The traffic warden, now rendered unconscious several times over, had been dumped into a skip full of building rubbish just off the Mile End Road. The lads had then driven to the waste ground behind Tom's lock-up for the transfer of the money and other goodies.

'All right. That's it, we're all done,'

announced Eddy, as Soap threw the last sack into the new van.

'You think it's a good idea taking it back to your place?' asked Soap.

'Well, number one — there's nowhere else we can keep it, and number two — it's the last place in the world they're going to look, ain't it?' reasoned Eddy.

'I suppose so,' said Soap begrudgingly, still not convinced of the wisdom of the plan.

'Anyway, fuck it. The battle's over, the war is won,' added Eddy optimistically.

For the first time in nearly a week, Eddy thought that he could see a future which didn't involve a violent and fingerless death. He reached into the back of the van, ripped open the side of a sack of weed and pulled out a handful. He passed the grass to Tom.

'Take this to Nick and let's get rid of it double quick. Tell him to hurry, okay?'

Tom nodded. 'I know where he'll be, I'll take it over there straight away.'

'What do we do?' asked Soap.

'Take all the gear and money back to mine and count out Harry's half a million,' said Eddy, cracking a smug fuck-off smile.

A little over an hour later, the sample of grass that Eddy had picked out was sitting on Rory Breaker's desk. Nick the Greek was sitting on the plush sofa waiting for Rory's verdict on the weed.

The scene was almost identical to Nick's last visit. One of Rory's helpers thrust a tall glass into Nick's hand and again he nodded his thanks. Behind Nick, more motor racing was playing on the bank of televisions that lined the entire wall.

Lenny, Rory's tall, dark and dangerous second-in-command came back into the room, having taken a sample of the weed for closer inspection.

'It's skunk all right,' Lenny assured Nick. 'And it's about as good as it gets.'

Rory toyed with the remote control that he was holding and then looked at Nick.

'Okay, we'll take it,' he decided, smelling the small plastic bag of grass. 'Half price.'

Nick, who had been sitting on the sofa quietly working out his commission on this deal, suddenly saw half of it disappear.

'I don't think he'll like that. You said three and a half thousand a key. That's what he wants, and you know that's a good price,' argued Nick.

'Yesterday I said three and a half grand, and today is today, if I'm not mistaken,' said Rory with extreme menace. 'I'll take it tomorrow for half price. If he wants to move it quick, he'll have to take it. Now look, I've got another race to watch in a minute, so if you'd be kind enough ...?' Rory pointed to the door.

''Course,' said Nick, reaching forward to put his glass on the table so he could leave. Rory's face had just enough time to register his obvious displeasure before Nick's drink fell through the empty table top and smashed on to the floor beneath.

Nick made a swift exit.

'Lenny, you and Nathan take this weed over to Snow White and the three little chemists. They should have a gander at this. I want a proper opinion,' ordered Rory.

'Yes, boss,' said Lenny, picking up the sample from the desk.

Rory turned up the volume on all his TVs and settled down to watch the race.

Lenny collected Nathan from downstairs and they drove over to what was known as Rory's House of Weed. The boys there would be able to give Rory an exact opinion of the worth of the weed he was about to buy.

As they walked up the flight of metal stairs that led from the street to the boys' house, the two men saw that the front door was ajar.

'Hang on, Lenny. Something smells bad,' said Nathan suspiciously.

'Yeah, your fucking aftershave,' commented Lenny. Then he too saw the half-open front door.

Shit. And neither of them were tooled up.

'Something's not quite right here. Go in slowly, Nathan,' ordered Lenny, cocking his ear to the sounds of movement and groaning coming from inside.

'Fuck you, funny man. You go in

first,' said Nathan.

'Just get the fuck in, will you?' insisted Lenny.

The two men edged forward together and pushed the door wide.

About ten feet inside, just the other side of the security cage, they saw a white male lying on the floor. The end of one of his legs ended in a bloody stump where the toes should have been.

'Lenny! For God's sake, help me. I'm in pain. I'm in so much pain. Jesus!' howled J when he spotted the pair.

'Jesus, what happened to you?' asked Lenny, starring down at the pool of blood surrounding J.

'We got hit! Some fuckers hit us and took everything!'

All of a sudden, Lenny's brain made certain, instant connections. Rory's House of Weed getting hit, plus Nick the Greek with a ton of weed to get rid of for a mysterious third party ...

Lenny realised that this added up to something that was going to get very nasty, very quickly.

# lock,stock
## & two smoking barrels

chapter ten

BACK AT EDDY and Bacon's place, the lads were enjoying the spoils of war. Bacon lay across the sofa, supported by a sea of overcoats, happily puffing on a large joint that he had taken from the seemingly infinite supply now stored in the back room. Tom sat at the table counting the fifties into piles of five thousand pounds, watched closely by Eddy and Soap.

'Not a bad day's work,' said Eddy. If he had been competing in the Understatement of the Year World Championships, he couldn't have come up with a better opener.

Just as one game of cards had turned their lives upside down in a few seconds, today's result against Dog had flipped it all back again. And it wasn't just the money and the drugs that made the lads feel so smug; it was the fact that they had pulled themselves out of the shit by their own bootlaces and given those thieving bastards next door a good kicking in the process.

'That pile takes care of Harry,' Eddy noted, running his fingers over a wad of money that made up slightly less that half of the total haul.

'How much is left over?' asked Soap, as casually as any question involving hundreds of thousands of pounds could be asked.

'Hold on — give us half a chance to count it,' mumbled Tom, mid-way through yet another bundle of notes.

'What about the gear?' said Soap, changing tack.

The mention of the wicked weed stirred Bacon out of his trance-like state. He looked over at Eddy and held out the remains of the joint he'd been smoking.

'Have a tug on that,' he invited.

'I don't want that horrible shit,

thanks very much,' refused Eddy. 'Give it to Soap.'

'I don't bloody want it,' shot back Soap.

As Tom reached the end of the bundle he was counting up and put it with the rest, Eddy came to a decision.

'Can we just lock up, and go and get very drunk now, please?' he proposed.

Next door, the scene was altogether grimmer. Now finally free from the gaffer tape and nursing their injuries, Dog and his gang were planning their next move.

Dog was angrier than Plank could ever remember seeing him in their long and tortuous relationship. The leader of this pack was out for blood and he was about to unleash his hounds.

Dog paced up and down the room, while John and Paul sat on the sofa, with Plank leaning against the wall next to them. They knew their orders would come soon enough.

'It was a bug. It must've been a fucking bug,' snarled Dog, his mind zipping through all the possibilities. 'The first thing I want you to do is search this house for bugs. And I mean I want you to strip it — every piece of furniture, every cupboard, every floorboard, right?'

He turned his angry glare on the gang. 'I want every inch of this fucking place examined with a fucking microscope,' decided Dog, getting keener with every word.

The others weren't so enthusiastic. But then, it was down to them to put Dog's grand schemes into action. Somehow their leader kept his paws clean of the really dirty work.

'What's the point in that?' piped up John, looking for an easy way out. 'Even if there was a bug, they'd have taken it with them.'

As Dog turned his glare on the speaker, Plank shot John a look which spoke volumes; he obviously thought John was both brave and foolish.

'It's a little late for you to start thinking,' growled Dog nastily. 'It's a possibility, and that's good enough for me. And after you strip the house, I want you to get every thieving slag this side of Ceylon and torture them ... badly!'

'We'll find them, Dog,' said Plank

unconvincingly.

Dog's eyes moved to Plank and fixed him like a rabbit caught in headlights.

'I know you will, because I want to know who is responsible. Otherwise, I will hold you responsible, clear?' he threatened. 'Now, get to work.'

The mood was no less bleak in Rory Breaker's office. Lenny and Nathan had returned, having spent the last few hours clearing up the mess at the grass laboratory. On their way they had dropped off J and Willy at the casualty unit of the nearest hospital. Unfortunately for them, the prognosis for the missing digits wasn't good.

Lenny and Nathan had then invited Winston to accompany them, so that he could explain what had happened to Rory himself. At first Winston had refused — until Lenny had made it clear that it was the kind of invitation that you couldn't refuse.

A rather shell-shocked and tired Winston was now standing between Lenny and Nathan, standing like a child up before the headmaster for a telling off.

True to form, Rory wasn't giving him an easy time.

'What about the security cage?' he snapped.

'The gates were locked, but they grabbed J and stuck a shotgun through,' Winston told him, looking pitifully sorry for himself. 'Poor bloody J got shot. It was a right mess.'

'Some girl took out one of them with a Bren gun,' said Lenny. 'Couldn't see who he was though — not enough of him left.'

'Good old Gloria,' added Winston, managing a half smile.

'It will cost you more than your life's worth if you jest with me,' retorted Rory, completely unamused.

'We shot one of them in the throat,' offered Winston, trying to redeem his position a little.

'What do you want — a fucking medal? I'll shoot you in the throat if I don't get my gear back,' threatened Rory. Then he paused, slightly confused, and asked, 'So the one you shot in the throat is the one in there now?'

'No, that's the one Gloria shot. We

got another one of them in the throat,'
said Winston.

The idea of higher casualties among
the enemy pleased Rory greatly.

'That's more like it. So where's the
one you shot in the throat?' he asked.

Winston shrugged. 'They took him
with them. He was still alive.'

'Still alive? How the fuck could he
be still alive?' shouted Rory. 'What did
you shoot him with? An air gun?'

There was an embarrassed pause,
with Winston looking more and more like
a schoolboy who'd been caught wanking
in the showers. He cleared his throat.

'We grow weed. We're not
mercenaries,' he said.

'You don't say,' sneered Rory. He
should have known better than to expect
these poncey shites to look after his
interests properly.

'Where do we start looking, Rory?'
queried Lenny rather unwisely.

Rory looked up, amazed at Lenny's
stupidity. It didn't take a mastermind to
work out what was going on.

'Mr Breaker! Today my name is Mr
Breaker,' Rory spat. 'You think this is a

coincidence? Some shite steals my goods, then thinks it is a good idea to sell it back to me. They've got less brains than you, Lenny. Get that greasy wop bastard Nick the Greek round here — if he's stupid enough to still be on this planet!'

'Yes, boss,' said Lenny, simply.

'I want him on that sofa now!' demanded Rory, gesticulating madly. 'And you, my chemist friend,' he added, pointing at Winston, 'are staying around until this mess is fixed. Understand?'

Winston managed a feeble nod.

That night was one of excessive drinking and extreme laddishness for Eddy and the lads. No known drinking game was left unplayed, no known alcoholic drink was left undrunk and the riotousness carried on until the small hours of the next morning.

When JD went to lock up at 3:00 am, he found the lads collapsed together in corner. Rather than wake them, he locked them in for the remainder of the night.

Not far away, Dog's gang had endured a most unpleasant night questioning and torturing local lowlifes, seeking information about the perpetrators of the ambush. But despite employing every dirty trick of interrogation and torture their vast experience could supply, their efforts revealed nothing — not even a sniff of who might have been responsible.

Next morning, just after dawn, they reported back to Dog, who was less than pleased with their failure.

'So we have a bit of a problem, don't we?' he said, scanning the uneasy faces of Plank, John and Paul, who were lined up against the far wall.

'Er ... well, yeah, we do,' agreed John, hesitantly.

'Yeah, we do,' repeated Dog. 'In fact it's a little more than a bit of a problem isn't it?'

Dog's voice was getting louder, and Plank knew that they were in for a bollocking that was going to be extreme even by Dog's standards.

'You could say that in the scale of these things this is the Mount-fucking-Everest of problems, couldn't you?' ranted Dog. 'And the reason it is such a mon-fucking-strosity of a problem, is because you don't have the first idea who did this to us, do you?'

Plank, who was desperately hoping that no one would remember that this job had been his idea in the first place, was tired and fed up.

'Dog, we've been up all night. It's no one from round here! We've had them all up against the wall. We shitted them right up, but no one knows anything,' he pleaded.

'If it was a local toerag we'd know by now. We weren't exactly gentle with them last night,' agreed John.

'We'd know,' chipped in Paul.

Dog had had more than he could take of their half-arsed excuses. His frustrations at the whole episode began to boil over as he started slapping Paul and John around the head by turns.

'You wouldn't know if it was the next-door fucking neighbours, you prick!' he howled. 'You find them, you hear me? And find them quick!'

Paul and John didn't wait to be told twice. They scarpered as quickly as they could, leaving the much smaller, rodent-like form of Plank as Dog's punch bag.

Suddenly remembering that this cock-up of a job had originally been Plank's idea, he began aiming his blows to the side of Plank's head.

'Now get out and start looking! Out! Out!' he screamed, completely losing it with the pathetic little runt. 'I'm sick of the sight of you, you little shit!'

Giving in completely to his temper, Dog grabbed Plank's shoulder's and threw him head first at the wall. At the mercy of momentum, Plank's small, weasely head hit an air vent and smashed straight through it.

Dazed and confused, Plank spat dust out of his mouth and tried to focus his spinning vision. As the scene slowed to a halt, he found himself wedged, with his head sticking out into next door's kitchen.

Plank blinked in confusion as he took in the huge pile of recording equipment, microphones and the reel-to-reel tape machine on the kitchen table under his noise. Then realisation finally dawned. Forgetting his pain and discomfort, he called back into the house behind.

'Dog? There's something here you ought to see.'

That morning, Nick the Greek had had a most upsetting alarm call. Lenny and Nathan had kicked in his door when it was barely light, and had dragged him almost screaming from his bed. Now he was standing in front of an excessively angry Rory Breaker and Nick still hadn't worked out why.

'Your stupidity might be your one saving grace,' Rory told him from a distance.

By now, Nick was quite petrified. Rory had a reputation as a psychotic of the first order and Nick knew that he wouldn't hesitate to inflict pain — or worse, if the mood took him. And from where Nick was standing, it looked like the mood was very much taking him.

'Err ...' Nick managed, before Rory interrupted.

'Don't fucking "er" me, Greek boy! How is it that your so-fucking-stupid, soon-to-be-dead friends thought they could steal my cannabis and then sell it back to me?' he yelled. 'Is this a declaration of war? Is this some sort of white cunts' joke that black cunts don't get? Because I am not fucking laughing, Nik-ol-as.'

Nick was horrified as the words hit home and he understood at last what had happened. Christ! That stupid bastard Tom had hit Rory's own House of Weed, then got Nick to try and sell it back to the evil fucker. Nick realised he was lucky to still be breathing this late in the morning.

'Nick, I have four interests in life,' Rory informed him. 'Motor racing, music, money and the annihilation of anyone who interferes with that shortlist. And you have just interfered with that shortlist.'

Nick swallowed hard as Rory continued.

'Now, I know that you couldn't have known the weed was mine, because even you are not so fucking stupid that if you did know, you would turn up here scratching your arse, with that 'what's going on here' look slapped across your Chevy Chase. But what you do know is where these people live.'

Rory got up from his desk and walked towards Nick, who was close to shitting himself.

'If you hold anything back, I'll kill you,' threatened Rory. 'If you bend the truth, or if I think you are bending the truth, I'll kill you. If you forget anything, I'll kill you. In fact, you're going to have to work very hard just to stay alive, Nick,' the man hissed, his face now only inches away from Nick's.

'Now, I hope you understand everything I have said?'

Nick nodded.

'Because if you don't, I'll kill you,' finished Rory quietly. 'Now, Mr Bubble and Squeak, you may enlighten me as to exactly who these fuckers think they are ...'

Nick spilled his guts.

Eddy's house was full of uninvited guests. Following Plank's sudden and painful discovery of the kitchen recording studio, Dog had smashed through the wall and ordered the gang to search the place. It didn't take long for them to find what they were looking for. On a table in the back room were the piles of fifty pound notes, just as Eddy and the boys had left them the night before.

John started counting the money, but gave up at half a million because there was simply too much.

'They've got all the cash,' he reported to Dog.

'And the puff,' added Paul.

The slags had to die, of course, but Dog had to admit to himself that he admired their nerve.

'Cheeky bastards. Count it,' ordered Dog.

'Shit Dog, there's a lot. Don't you want to take it next door?' protested John.

'We're not going next door until we've flayed these dead men walking,' stated Dog. 'Pass the money here — I'll count it out the back. The rest of you find somewhere to hide. I don't want them seeing you as soon as they walk in.'

'We've got their shooters here as well,' said John, brandishing the two ancient hammer-lock guns that Eddy and the lads had used.

'That means they'll most likely be unarmed when they get back, stupid fuckers. Pass me those guns — you lot use your own, okay?' ordered Dog, grabbing both muskets. 'Now hide and get ready.

Wait until they're all inside, then give it to them.'

Dog headed into the back room and began work on the piles of money, while Plank started looking for a hiding place.

At that precise moment, Dog's intended victims were sitting at JD's bar nursing four phenomenal hangovers. The lads stared down into their coffees, somehow hoping that the smell would stop the pounding in their heads.

The conversation had turned to the subject of selling the weed, and the potential problems of pulling off a major drug deal when they didn't have a fucking clue what they were doing.

'*Scarface*. I've seen that film *Scarface*,' offered Bacon. 'If you want to know how to do a drug deal properly, then we should watch *Scarface*.'

'That really inspires confidence, that does,' noted Eddy.

'Anyway,' Tom began, 'this guy Rory Breaker ...'

'The psychotic black dwarf with an Afro?' interrupted Soap.

'That would be the man, yes,' said Tom.

'I've heard about him. He's a fucking lunatic,' said Soap.

'You don't half moan all the fucking time, don't you?' remarked Tom. 'Anyway, Rory Breaker can afford to do the deal at the price we are selling. It's not worth him giving us trouble. He knows we would be a pain in the arse, and who wants a pain in the arse?'

'I'd take a pain in the arse for half a million,' disagreed Soap.

'You'd take a pain in the arse for air miles.'

'Tom — the fatter you get, the sadder you get.'

Eddy raised his hand.

'Jesus, would you two ladies stop flirting for one minute? After we pay Hatchet his money, this deal puts us up near enough two hundred thousand pounds each. Not bad for a day's work, I think you'll agree,' he said.

'Anyway, we'll give the weed to Nick the Greek and he can do the dealing with Rory Breaker, so we're well out of it,' finished Tom.

Nick the Greek was pacing up and down

inside his own lock-up wondering what the fuck to do next. Outside, one of Rory's little helpers was standing guard to make sure that Nick didn't do a runner — which was exactly what he felt like doing. Anyway Nick looked at it, he was badly in the shit.

If it had been Tom that had hit Rory's House of Weed, then Tom was a good deal tastier than he'd been letting on and Nick was for it. If it wasn't Tom, then Tom was about to die for no reason and Nick was still right back in the shit.

Nick's phone rang and he jerked it open nervously.

'Yeah?'

'That's no way to answer your phone,' said a high-pitched voice with a Scouse accent.

'Is that you, Dean?'

'No, it's Lord fucking Lucan,' replied the Scouser.

'What can I do for you, Dean? This is really not a good time,' stated Nick flatly, resuming his pacing.

'You know those shotguns I sold you? Well I need them back,' Dean told him.

'Not likely, I'm afraid. I don't think I'll be seeing them again,' said Nick.

'I've got the money to pay for them,' offered Dean.

'I'm sure you have, but I don't think you understand. I'm not likely to see the guns or the people I sold them to again,' Nick insisted, his mind once again turning to thoughts of Tom and his soon-to-be violent end.

Nick flipped his mobile phone shut, cutting off the connection.

Dean looked across at Gary.

'Well, if we can't get them, we can't get them,' he shrugged.

Barry the Baptist, however, had a rather different idea when he heard the bad news.

'You fucking well have to get them!' he yelled down the phone when Dean reported in.

'But we made a deal for everything inside the cabinet, and we brought you that lot,' Dean reminded him, trying to reason his way out of the situation.

Barry wasn't having any of it.

'Inside, out-fucking-side, I don't give a shit. You get those guns, because if you don't ...'

'Yeah, Bazza, then what?' said Dean, nudging Gary to alert him to his brave new stand.

'Have you heard of Harry Lonsdale?' rasped Barry down the line. 'Otherwise known as Hack-you-up-with-a-Hatchet Harry, infamous for his removal of people's digits?'

Dean swallowed hard and a look of panic transformed his face.

'Well, this is a "James Bond, need to know" time,' Barry told him. 'You were getting those guns for him; he fucking wants them, and he fucking wants them now! When you dance with the devil you wait for the song to stop, know what I mean?'

The line went silent for a moment while, over in Harry's office, Barry passed the phone across to his boss. Dean listened in terror at the other end as Harry Hatchet took the phone and spoke into the receiver very gently.

'Do you know who I am? I am split in two,' came the insidious voice. 'There is me, and there is my patience, and my patience has gone to hospital. You are not far behind, know what I mean?'

There was a short, menacing pause before Harry continued. 'I want you to find those guns, get whoever's got them, torture them, kill them, and bring back what belongs to me. Because if you don't, you and your families are bang in trouble!'

Harry slammed down the phone and Dean looked across at Gary with sheer horror on his face.

'Who was that?' asked Gary, who had recently rejoined the real world and was alarmed by the direction the conversation seemed to have taken.

'That was Horrible Hatchet Harry, on the line him-fucking-self!' reported Dean.

'Jesus! I've heard about him.'

'Yeah, well, we're right in the shite. They were his fucking guns that we sold to Nick, and he wants them back,' grimaced Dean. 'We've got to find them, Gary.'

Dean redialled Nick's number just as before, and the ringing was answered immediately by a nervous-sounding Nick the Greek.

'Listen, no fucking about, Nick.

Where can I find those guns?'

Rory Breaker checked the ammunition in
his guns and decided they were ready for
the job in hand. He was sitting in the
back of a large, white van accompanied by
Winston and seven of the most heavily-
armed men in London. They were
driving toward the address that Nick had
provided, and Rory was out for blood.
Lots of blood.

'We are going to do a proper
decoration job,' he announced. 'I want
the grey skies of London illuminated. I
want that house painted red. Winston
here is coming along to see if he can
recognise any of the fuckers.'

Winston looked around the interior
of the van and wondered why fate had
consigned him to such a terrible destiny.
These days it seemed his lot was always to
be surrounded by mentally unstable men
with guns.

Rory's van turned into Eddy's street,
driving past a tall man dressed in black
who was just stepping out of his car.

'Wait here, son,' ordered Big Chris to
his offspring. He was heading to Eddy's to

collect Harry's money.

At the other end of the street, another car pulled into view, driving slowly along the kerb until it came to rest a few hundred yards from Eddy's place.

'This is where Nick said those fucking guns were,' said a Scouse accent.

'What do we do now?'

'Fucking wait, you dipstick,' said Dean. 'Wait for someone to come out or go in.'

At that moment, Dean caught sight of the white van that was backing quickly towards the front door of the address Nick had given them. Not for the first time that day, he wondered what the fuck was going on.

Inside Eddy's house, Dog's gang heard the van pull up outside. Plank signalled to the others to get into their hiding places, then he slid under the sofa again, his gun at the ready.

Outside, the van's rear doors opened, and Rory's troops streamed out. Rory, with a gun in each hand, kicked open the door and burst through, quickly followed by his men, each of them brandishing a large machine gun.

Rory peered around the room, but no one seemed to be home. He walked inside.

From his position under the sofa, Plank saw the men begin to search the place.

'What the fuck is going on here?' Plank wondered to himself, squeezing back the trigger of his own long shotgun. Why had the gang broken into their own home?

Eddy's house now contained two rival gangs of heavily-armed and extremely evil motherfuckers.

It was a time-bomb waiting to explode, and Plank was right in the middle of it. His brow broke out in beads of sweat and his hands started to shake slightly.

One of Rory's men approached the sofa, his machine gun sweeping back and forth before him. His shiny black shoes were now only inches from Plank's twitching face.

'Oh, fucking hell!' muttered Dog under his breath.

The only thing in the entire house more nervous than Plank was his trigger finger.  Plank watched the numerous pairs of shoes moving around until he could stand the tension no longer.  His shaking finger eased down on the trigger until finally, finally the silence was broken by the sound of a gunshot ...

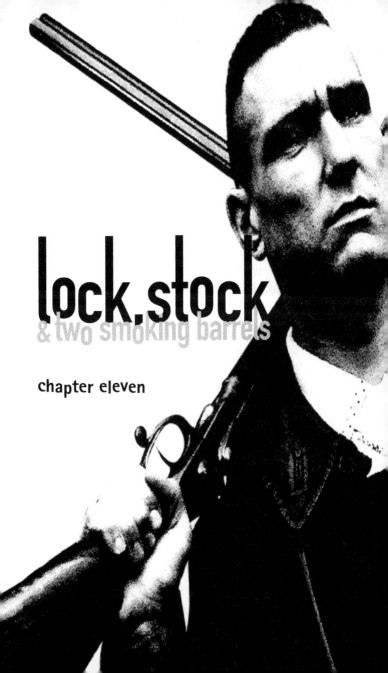

# lock,stock
## & two smoking barrels

**chapter eleven**

DRIVING BACK FROM JD's bar towards home in Eddy's car, the lads were still on a high. The air was blue as they tried to out do each other with a series of ever more disgusting jokes. Over the worst part of their hangovers now, they were looking forward to getting Harry off their backs by making the payment that was due today, and also to moving out the weed at enormous profit to each of them.

'There's six black cocks sitting on the side of the road. How many beaks have they got between them?' asked Tom, starting yet another joke.

'Six,' said Soap, playing the straight man for this one.

'And how many wings have they got between them?'

What Eddy and the lads didn't know was the number of people either dead or currently dying in their very own front room.

After Plank's first twitching gunshot, the entire place had erupted into a bloodbath. The windows were blown out from inside with the initial round of fire from dead Mick's Bren gun, now in John's possession. Altogether, six semi-automatic machine guns, five shotguns and four hand guns were discharged within the confines of the small front room, resulting in a carnival of dead flesh.

As soon as the shooting started Dog, alarmed by the magnitude and length of the battle since he was expecting the new arrivals to be unarmed, sneaked a peek from his hiding place in the back room. As he opened the adjoining door he was struck in the face by a large splattering of blood and entrails. Deciding instantly that discretion was the better part of valour, Dog legged it.

He grabbed the bag of money and the two old hammer-lock guns, and opened the large side doors to the building that was Eddy's home. Throwing the bag of money down to the street five feet below, he checked behind him, then jumped down himself with a gun in each hand.

Dog looked back at the building where Plank and the rest of his gang were being shot into tiny pieces and smiled. He was well out of it. When he turned round, holding the old guns, one in each hand like a Mexican bandit, he found himself looking straight into the extremely unpleasant face of Big Chris.

Big Chris had been watching the house from across the street, intrigued and fascinated by the arrival of the white van and the disgraceful violence that had followed its appearance.

'Got something here for me, have you?' asked Big Chris.

Dog looked stunned — who the fuck was this?

'Come on, chop chop,' added the big man.

Before Dog had a chance to use the

shotguns, Chris grabbed one in each hand and delivered a swift but brutal headbutt to Dog's forehead. Dog went down like a ton of bricks.

Chris picked up the bag of money and walked away.

'Thank you very much,' he said to himself. Getting Harry's half a million had been easier than expected and had been accomplished without the need for very much unpleasantness.

Big Chris opened the front door of his car where Little Chris was waiting inside.

'Wrap up those guns and check that money, son,' he ordered. 'And put your safety belt on.'

Waiting along the street, Dean and Gary had seen Big Chris suddenly reappear from the direction of Ed's house. They immediately recognised the two guns.

'He's got the guns. Go ahead and get them,' urged Dean, nudging Gary's elbow.

'Why me?'

Gary didn't like the look of Big Chris at all and wasn't in a hurry to approach the man.

'You're supposed to be the hard case. You go and get the guns!' argued Dean.

'I drive the fucking car,' said Gary, pointing stubbornly at the steering wheel in front of him.

'Oh, just get the guns, Gary,' appealed Dean again.

'I'm not getting the fucking guns! You get the fucking guns. You're all fucking mouth, you!' yelled Gary, losing his rag.

As they argued, Big Chris' car pulled away from the kerb.

'Quick, follow him! We've got to get those guns or we're dead,' yelped Dean.

Gary started the engine and set off in pursuit.

Across the way, Dog regained consciousness and wandered out into the road in a rather confused state — straight into the path of an oncoming car. Panicked by the collision, the driver raced away.

Groaning slightly, Dog collected his bloodied and bruised body and mind together and stepped out into the road once more, flagging down another car.

This time the driver stopped because Dog was blocking the road.

Without waiting to introduce himself, Dog reached in through the driver's open window and grabbed the man's throat, dragging him from the car. Then Dog jumped inside and set off after Big Chris, determined to find the bastard. As far as Dog was concerned, that money was his.

Back in Eddy's place, a strange silence hung over the battlefield now littered with corpses. Most of the floor space was taken up with dead bodies, with a few also scattered tastefully across the odd table-top and sofa. Gun smoke hung thick in the air like an evil smog.

Among the wreckage there were just two people on their feet. Winston, who had survived because he had hidden in the van, and Rory Breaker, who had survived because he was a psychotic black dwarf with an Afro, and a fucking lunatic to boot.

They were preparing to leave, with Winston throwing bags of weed into the rear of the van.

'That's one of them,' said Winston, as

he stepped over Plank's blood-stained body.

'Lucky, that,' said Rory snidely.

'He's the one we shot in the neck,' added Winston, picking up the last two bags.

'Is that right, Mr Botanical?'

A faint moan came from the near-dead body of Plank and Rory took out his gun preparing to finish the job. He kicked over Plank's body with his foot, intending to shoot him in the face. But as Plank was spun around, Rory saw that he was still holding a loaded shotgun in his hands.

As Winston reached the front door, he heard the sound of two guns being fired simultaneously, followed by the thud of Rory's body falling to the floor.

Without looking back, Winston threw the last of the weed into the van, got in the driver's seat and drove like fuck, desperate to get away from the house of horrors and the nightmare of the last twenty-four hours. Swerving Rory's white van around the corner, he nearly hit a car coming into the street. The vehicles flew past each other with barely a fag end between them.

'Jesus!' exclaimed Tom, looking back from the other car. 'He was in a fucking hurry!'

Eddy parked the car and the four lads climbed out. It took them all of one — millionth of a second to spot that something was very wrong.

'I don't believe this,' said Bacon, peering in through the broken glass of the front windows. Inside he could see smoke.

Smoke and bodies — lots of bodies.

'What the fuck has been going on?' he asked.

'Jesus Christ!' said Eddy.

'What about the money? The gear?' panicked Soap.

Tom was the first one inside. Close up it was even more of a bloody mess than was apparent through the window. He looked around, but it didn't need a genius to see that both the weed and cash were gone.

'That's fucked it!' he said, stunned. 'What do we do now? There's no money and no weed. It's all been replaced by a pile of corpses.'

'Okay, don't panic. Let's think about

this,' said Soap, as if he were trying to solve a clue in *The Times* crossword puzzle.

'Bollocks!' spat Eddy. 'You can think about it for as long as you like — but I'm off, mate!'

Big Chris climbed the flight of stairs to Harry's office with the heart-warming sense of a job well done and of a debt well-collected.

Coming out of Harry's at the top of the stairs he caught sight of John O'Driscoll, a man he had last seen sprawled unconscious under a sunlamp. As O'Driscoll got nearer, Chris saw that most of the skin on his face and neck was a hideous red colour, and was peeling off in great chunks leaving bright pink tissue exposed underneath.

'Hello, John. Nice holiday?'

O'Driscoll wasn't amused.

'I won't be seeing you again, Chris. I've paid him every last penny,' he said.

'I'm sure you have. No one was accusing you of being dishonest, John,' Chris assured him as they passed on the stairs.

'Is that you Chris?' Harry's voice called from inside the office.

Big Chris walked straight inside, putting the guns down in the middle of the desk and the bag of money next to them. Harry put down the vagina-shaped penis massager he was fondling and picked up one of the weapons, immediately realising that these were the guns he'd ordered Barry to obtain.

'How did you get your hands on these?' asked Harry, gobsmacked.

'The boys had them. I know you like these things, so I wondered if you wanted them,' explained Chris.

It was evident that Chris hadn't known Harry was looking for these particular guns, but had brought them as an offering anyway.

'Err ... Yeah, sure, I'll have them,' he nodded, making it sound as if he was doing Chris a favour.

'Was it hard work getting the money?' rasped Barry from his usual position on the sofa.

'Not especially,' said Chris, honestly, 'but I had to upset a few people doing it.'

'Have you counted it?' asked Harry,

still admiring the shotguns.

'Yeah, it's all there, to the pound.'

'So, they were going to pay, then.' mused Harry.

Chris weighed up the likelihood in his mind.

'Looks like it, but who knows? The opportunity to collect it was there. And in my experience, it's best to take that opportunity ... if it is there.'

Harry reached inside his jacket and took out a white envelope which he gave to Chris.

'Good work.'

Big Chris slid the envelope into his jacket, nodded his thanks and left. Outside, he made his way towards his car, oblivious to the fact that he was being watched from across the street by the Scousers.

'He must have left the guns inside. We gotta get them,' insisted Dean.

Gary grimaced. 'This is dangerous shit, Dean. We don't even know who lives in there,' he warned.

'Listen, I don't care who lives there, but it's got to be preferable to death by Hatchet. Come on, let's get the fucking thing over with,' said Dean, getting out of the car.

The Scousers crossed the street and entered the doorway that Chris had exited from. As they did, they passed a large bronze sign which read:

---

**HARRY LONSDALE
PORN KING**

---

Neither of them stopped to read it ...

Just a few minutes' car drive away, Eddy and the boys were parked up, trying to decide what to do next.

'I don't think that's the right move,' insisted Soap.

'It's either appeal to Harry, sell him my old man's bar, or we lose a digit daily. I'm going to call Harry,' decided Eddy.

'As if he'll care,' put in Bacon.

'He won't care about us — but it was his money that someone just stole from us, and he'll care about that all right. Pass me your phone,' Eddy told Tom.

'Think about what you're going to

say, Ed. We are on very thin ice,' said Bacon.

'You don't fucking say?' said Eddy, starting to dial.

Inside Harry's building, the Scousers were creeping up the staircase when they heard the phone ring in the office above them.

Harry, still playing gleefully with his new guns, picked it up.

'Is that you, boy?'

'It's Ed, if that's what you mean,' said the voice on the other end of the line.

'It's pay day, ain't it?' said Harry, sitting himself on the edge of his desk.

'Yeah, I wanted to talk to you about that.'

'I bet you did. I've got half a million nicker sitting here in front of me, which means some poor sod doesn't. You must have really upset a few people getting that, boy,' Harry chuckled, sliding a pair of cartridges into the musket. 'But that isn't really my concern, is it? What does concern me is the guns you had. I want to talk to you about that — so get your arse over to my office now. And I do mean now.'

Never one for long goodbyes — or indeed, goodbyes of any length — Harry put the phone down.

'Well?' said Bacon.

As Eddy stared into the silent receiver, his state of shock was obvious to the rest of the lads in the car. He handed back Tom's mobile phone.

'Well, what?' answered Eddy eventually, his mind still reeling from what Harry had said.

'Well, what did he say?' asked Tom, impatiently.

'He said he thinks we have already paid him, and he wants to see us in his office so we can talk about those guns,' reported Eddy.

'You what? What are you on about?' spluttered Soap, confused.

Eddy's brain was working fast, trying to make sense of it all.

'Listen, if he has those old guns, he might have got his hands on the money. I think we should go and see him.'

Going to see Hatchet Harry did not sound like a very safe plan to the others.

'I think you're a sandwich short of a

picnic, mate. You want to start making sense,' stated Bacon.

Eddy started up the engine.

'We're going,' he said simply.

In the hall outside Harry's office, Gary and Dean had reached the door and were preparing to make their move. Gary waited to one side, while Dean kicked open the door and advanced, holding a gun in each hand.

As he looked inside, a thousand ugly thoughts flew through Dean's troubled mind. Then he froze with horror as he found himself confronted by a man holding a long shotgun standing only a few feet away from him.

Hatchet Harry looked up and realised that the short man standing in the doorway with a gun in each hand had probably not come to deliver the mail. His finger tightened around the trigger of the musket.

Dean and Harry stood staring at each other, neither daring to move a muscle.

Then Harry swung the gun round quickly and fired. The blast hit Dean in the chest, and the sheer force of the impact blew the Scouser up into the air, propelling him out into the hallway where he hit the wall and slumped to the floor covered in blood. Just to be sure, Harry emptied the other barrel into Dean's stomach, creating another wide and bloody wound.

Dean's spectacular demise had been watched by Gary, who now flung himself into the room. He walked towards Harry at the desk, firing his two guns as rapidly as he could.

'You fucking bastard!' screamed Gary.

Harry took the first shot in his shoulder, and the next six in his chest, toppling backwards over the desk.

Gary, devastated by the sudden atrocity that had befallen Dean, carried on shooting into Harry's now-dead body from point blank range.

Sitting on the sofa by the far wall, Barry the Baptist picked up the steel hatchet that adorned Harry's desk. He threw it across the room, scoring a fatal hit in Gary's back. Gary's arm bent round, instinctively firing his last shot at his assailant.

As Gary turned around and collapsed

on to his knees, he saw Barry sitting on the sofa, now with a major bullet wound in his abdomen.

Gary's eyes widened in confusion and horror.

'What the fuck are you doing here?' he blurted out, before collapsing to the floor, dead.

'What the fuck are you doing here?' responded Barry.

In the last few seconds of Barry the Baptist's life, he realised what had happened. But it was far to late to do anything about it.

Eddy's car pulled up in front of Harry's building, and the four lads looked up to the windows of the hatchet man's office, knowing that their fate rested in the old bastard's hands.

'You and me, Tom. Come on,' said Eddy getting out of the car.

Tom reluctantly obeyed.

'What do you mean me? Why me?' he protested, as he followed Eddy up the stairs.

As they approached the doorway, they saw Dean's body slumped against the wall.

'Jesus!'

Inside the office they found three more corpses. Gary — though they had no idea who he was — face down on the floor with a hatchet in his back; Barry the Baptist, dead on the sofa with a stomach wound; and Hatchet Harry himself, shot to pieces behind his own antique desk.

'Not a-fucking-gain,' groaned Eddy, staring at the bodies. This surfeit of corpses was beginning to give him the arsehole.

'What the fuck has happened here?' said Tom quietly, then decided, 'That's it, I'm off.'

Eddy, however, had spotted something. Sitting on the middle of Harry's desk was a bag of money. Their bag of money.

'That, Tom, is our money,' he said, knowing that voicing his thought would make it true.

Eddy tiptoed towards the desk as if he was scared of waking the dead.

'Ed, come on,' appealed Tom, eager to get out as soon as possible.

Summoning all his courage, Eddy grabbed the bag and lifted it off the desk.

None of the corpses littering the office stirred. No one was going to stop him.

'This is our money, Tom,' he said again, proudly.

Now the bag was in Eddy's hands, the thought of taking it with them suddenly seemed the obvious thing to do. Then Tom spotted his precious old guns, dropped from where the mighty figure of Hatchet Harry had fallen.

'I'll meet you in the car, I'm getting the guns as well,' said Tom. 'I'll only be a minute — see you down there.'

Eddy left with the cash and headed down the stairs, straight back to where the others were waiting in the car.

It had taken Big Chris five minutes to walk back to his car and as he approached it he saw the face of Little Chris sitting in the passenger seat. For some reason, he didn't look all that happy.

Big Chris opened the door and climbed in.

'A job well done, son. Made a few quid out of that one,' he said cheerfully.

There was no reply.

'Son?'

Big Chris looked around — just as Dog leapt up from his hiding place in the rear seat. He was holding a knife to the boy's throat.

'Where is what I want?' he demanded.

Big Chris made a rapid assessment of the situation. There was nothing he could do at the moment.

'You all right back there, mate?' he smiled.

'Very fucking funny. Where's the money?' snarled Dog, moving the sharp edge of the blade closer to the boy's neck.

'It's in the office. I just left it in the office,' Big Chris told him.

'Well, you'd better go and get it from the office. That's if you want your son to reach his next birthday. Now, chop-fucking-chop.'

Big Chris glanced over at his son, checking that he was wearing his seat belt, then he slipped on his own. He put the car key into the ignition and started the engine.

'What are you doing?'

'Well, it's a five minute walk or a thirty second drive. I could have parked outside, but I might have got a ticket. I don't suppose that matters now,' explained Big Chris, pulling away from the kerb and gathering speed.

Eddy sat in the driving seat of his car, with Bacon and Soap in the back. On Eddy's lap was the bag of money from Harry's office.

'Where's Tom?' asked Bacon.

'He's getting the guns. He'll be down in a second,' replied Eddy, lifting out a pile of fifty pound notes and flicking through them.

'Well, what's going on then?' said Soap.

'I don't know,' grinned Eddy. 'But what I do know is that there's no more Harry, which means there's no more debt. And if there's no more debt, there's no more problem.'

The others hung on his every word as Eddy thought it through.

'And there's no more problem with our neighbours because they're all dead. I think, if I get this right, we haven't done anything wrong, which means we are in the clear,' Eddy finished triumphantly.

Eddy's thoughts were rudely cut

short as a car suddenly smashed violently into the rear of the parked vehicle, caving in the rear wing and knocking the three lads unconscious.

Big Chris had picked up speed during the short drive to Harry's office. Knowing that Dog was the only one not wearing a safety belt, he had deliberately pulled hard to the right and rammed the nearest parked vehicle.

The two smashed cars lay silent for several seconds, then Big Chris shook himself and clambered out of his seat. Opening a rear door, he dragged out Dog who was still unconscious. Then, face contorting with rage, Big Chris began slamming the car door on the bastard's head. He delivered blow after blow after blow, each one harder than the last.

'Never, never, not as long as I can remember,' Big Chris screamed, 'has anybody been as fucking rude to me as you have.'

Little Chris climbed from the wrecked car unhurt and came round to ask if he could have a go at shutting the door on Dog. It might be a useful part of his training.

'In a moment, son.'

When Dog was quite, quite, quite dead, Big Chris went to check on the status of the poor bastards in the car that he had been forced to ram. He didn't like involving innocent bystanders, but what else could he do?

'All right, mate?' asked Big Chris, leaning in at the open driver's window. Then he saw the familiar bag containing Harry's money sitting on the unconscious Eddy's lap. He didn't know how it had got there, but he knew where it belonged.

'Cheeky little bastard,' said Big Chris, snatching the bag from the car.

Big Chris headed straight into Harry's building to return the money. Halfway up the stairs he spotted the corpse of Dean propped up against the wall just outside the office. This didn't look good.

Stepping over Dean's corpse, Big Chris walked into Harry's office just as Tom freed the shotguns from under Harry's remains.

Now, this was an embarrassing position for Tom to be in. Chris had to respect the fact that Tom was holding what appeared to be a pair of loaded shotguns. Tom had to respect the fact that they were not loaded.

Without anybody losing too much face, Tom left through the side exit of the building with the guns and Big Chris left with the bag of money tucked under his arm.

Everybody else got arrested.

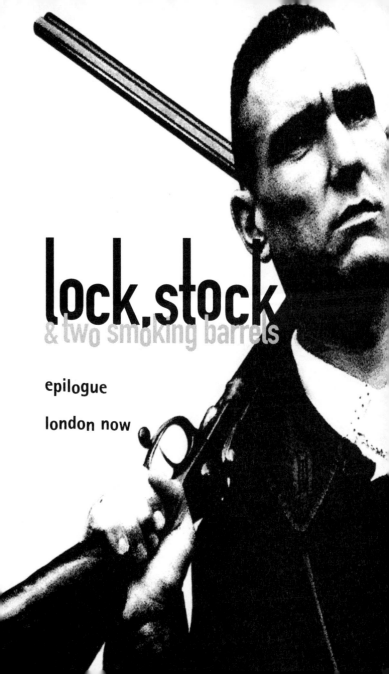

lock,stock
& two smoking barrels

epilogue

london now

EDDY REACHED FORWARD to scoop up the huge wad of notes and coins that were sitting obediently on the table in front of him.

'Odds chaps. You got to remember the odds,' he advised, as if it was all an unfortunate misunderstanding between gentlemen. He started counting his winnings.

The door to the small room flew open as a man in the familiar blue of a police uniform burst inside. He took in the situation immediately.

'I hope I'm not interrupting,' snarled

the sergeant.

The two junior policemen playing cards at the table with Eddy leapt to their feet, red-faced with embarrassment, and stood to attention.

'Comfortable, Edward?' asked the sergeant moving slowly across the interrogation room towards where Eddy was now sitting alone. Eddy ran his fingers through the wad of notes in his hand, causing the two policemen to twitch uneasily.

'Considering I haven't slept for forty-eight hours, that I've got a dozen broken ribs, a black eye, and I can feel a case of the flu coming on, I ...'

'All right. All right,' interrupted the sergeant. 'Don't think that I wouldn't like to get rid of you, but before I can there's a little matter that needs clearing up. I've got nineteen shot, stabbed and generally mutilated dead bodies scattered over various parts of London. And what I need to know, son, is what the fuck's been going on?'

Eddy fixed the sergeant straight in the eyes.

'If you think you're in the dark,' said Eddy, 'I'm in a black hole blindfolded.'

Then Eddy went back to counting his money.

Outside the interrogation room, the police sergeant rejoined his colleagues. Three policemen and one rather bruised traffic warden were watching Eddy through the half open door.

'No, he's not one of them,' said the traffic warden shakily.

The sergeant looked at his fellow officers with deep frustration, but there was nothing more they could do.

'Get him out of here,' ordered the sergeant. 'Turn him loose.'

When Eddy walked through the double swing door of the police station back into the free world, the first thing he saw was the welcome sight of Alan's face. However, JD's barman had some less than welcome news for him.

'I think your dad would like a word with you, Ed,' he said, pointing across to where Eddy recognised his father's car waiting in the station's car park.

'Where are the others?' asked Eddy.

'They got out yesterday,' Alan told him, taking a drag of his cigarette. 'They're waiting for you back at the bar.'

Eddy, nursing a plaster on his forehead, headed down the station's white stone steps towards JD's car. When he reached the vehicle, he opened the passenger door and climbed in next to his father.

'All right, Dad?' he asked, resignation in his voice.

'I'm all right, how about yourself?' replied JD, leaning across to get a better look at the state of his son.

'Oh, I'm all right. I could do with a drink, though,' said Eddy, nearly managing a smile.

'All in good time,' said JD, but he wasn't really here to find out how Eddy was doing. 'So, you in the clear then? More importantly, am I?'

'It appears so,' nodded Eddy, stating what he believed to be an accurate summary of what was, after all, a very complicated situation.

'Appears so? You'll have to do better than fucking appears so, my boy,' demanded JD.

Eddy took a breath. He was used to a hard time from the old sod.

'Well, everyone's dead, Dad. I think that's about as clear as it gets. Now how about that drink?' Eddy was desperate for the parental interrogation to be over.

'You know where the bar is,' commented JD.

'Eh?'

'Don't get too comfortable — Alan's got to sit there,' explained JD, indicating the seat where Eddy's backside was currently parked. 'You, my son, are lucky you're still breathing, let alone walking. I suggest you take full advantage of that fact.'

'Cheers, Dad,' sighed Eddy, climbing out of the car.

When Eddy finally arrived at JD's bar, Bacon, Tom and Soap greeted him with a mixture of relief and concern.

'You took your time. Where have you been?' asked Bacon.

'Let me sit down and I'll tell you,' said Eddy, nearly collapsing into one of the large booths at the back of the bar. He took a long, long drink of cold, imported beer, then ran through his recent experiences with the rozzers.

'The traffic warden went to the morgue and recognised the neighbours' bodies, which put us in the clear. They've got no case against us, because there's no evidence against us,' grinned Eddy. 'The only thing linking us with any of it is those shotguns.'

'And Tom took care of them, didn't you?' said Bacon.

Tom looked a little embarrassed — an expression the lads knew only too well. It meant that Tom was hiding something.

'You did take care of the guns, didn't you Tom?' demanded Soap.

'I wanted to talk to you about that,' he said, looking even more uncomfortable.

'Well, talk,' snapped Bacon.

'Well, actually, they're sitting in the car. I thought we might sell them back to Nick the Greek, but I'm having a bit of a problem getting hold of him,' Tom told them.

This news was not received well by the rest of the table.

'You dippy bastard!' spat Bacon.

'So the only item that at all connects us with the crime is sitting in the boot of your car parked outside?' yowled Eddy, incredulous.

'They cost seven hundred quid. They're hardly likely to trace them back to us,' argued Tom.

'Do you think it's worth taking the risk for seven hundred quid?' demanded Soap.

'Tom, you're a dick,' announced Eddy. 'Now, you take those guns and throw them off the nearest bridge into the Thames,' he ordered.

'And throw yourself off while you're at it,' added Bacon.

'Now, Tom!' insisted Soap.

With a look of regret on his face, Tom got up from the table. He hadn't taken more than two or three steps when he turned around, ready to make another appeal.

'Now!' chorused the other three in perfect unison before he could open his mouth.

Tom knew that this was an argument he was not going to win and slowly trudged out of the bar.

'Can I have another beer, please, Dad?' Eddy called from the booth.

'I'm busy, get it yourself,' came the curt reply from the bar.

Eddy emptied the last dregs from his bottle. When he put it down he found that Soap and Bacon were staring at a figure walking towards them across the bar. It was Big Chris.

The boys shrank down slightly in their seats. Shit.

Big Chris came up to their booth and placed a bag on the table. It looked somewhat familiar.

'It seems that Hatchet Harry under-estimated you lot, and that seems to have cost him,' he said, looking directly at Eddy. 'I am not going to make the same mistake, am I? So I decided to bring your bag back.'

The lads sat in stunned silence, staring at the bag.

'The words you are looking for are "thank you",' suggested Chris.

'Thank you,' parroted Eddy.

'Now, you have presented me with a problem. I've lost my employer, so I've taken care of myself and my son. If you think that's unfair you just come and pay me a little visit: but you'd better be waving the white flag high and clear so I can see it or it will be the last visit you ever make. You understand?'

The boys managed a little nod each.

'One more thing,' added Big Chris.

The lads looked at the bag they had

never expected to see again, then up at Chris.

'It's been emotional,' he said.

Chris walked out into the dark street where Little Chris was waiting in a shiny new sports car.

'That takes care of that lot. We are now officially in the money-loaning business.'

He started the engine. 'Put your seatbelt on, son. We're out of here.'

Back in JD's bar, Eddy ripped open the bag and searched its insides.

'It's empty!'

'What do you mean?' queried Soap.

'I mean it's fucking empty!' said Eddy, clarifying things.

Surely Big Chris wouldn't go to all that effort, only to torture them further by handing over an empty bag.

Bacon lunged forward and looked inside the bag for himself. He stuck his hand inside and pulled out a brown envelope. He looked over at Ed, puzzled.

Less than three minutes' drive away, Tom had parked his car and was taking the old muskets out of the boot. He gave one of them a last, loving stroke and then wrapped them in a piece of cloth and tried to walk casually towards the edge of the bridge.

Eddy ripped open the top of the envelope and pulled out a Christies auction brochure.

'What the fuck is this?'

Soap started hurriedly flicking through its pages.

On the bridge, Tom leaned over the edge and looked down into the murky waters of the River Thames. Then, with as little fuss as possible, he let go of the cloth bundle in his arms and regretfully watched it disappear over the edge.

In the bar, Soap was flicking through the pages that showed shotgun after antique shotgun. Finally he found a pair of impressive hammer-lock shotguns that he recognised rather well.

His eyes stared down at their estimated value, '£250,000 – £300,000 each,' read the catalogue.

'Fucking, fucking, fucking hell!'

And Tom was about to throw them into the river.

'What's his number?' demanded Eddy, pulling his mobile phone out of his coat pocket. Bacon and Soap both scrabbled for theirs, and all three began dialling their best guess at Tom's number.

On the bridge, Tom paused and decided to check that the guns had reached the river. Leaning over the handrail he saw that instead of falling to the water, the guns had become lodged on a small ledge. He climbed up on to the hand rail of the bridge so that he could push them over properly.

At the bar, Eddy had decided he should be the one to make the call.

'Don't you jam the line, I'll call him,' he ordered, dialling Tom's number. Halfway through the digits the phone went dead.

'My fucking batteries!' cursed Eddy.

Soap started punching in Tom's number.

'I'll call him!' insisted Eddy, making a grab for the mobile.

'Fuck off! I'll dial, tell me the number,' argued Soap.

Eddy ignored him and made another grab for Soap's phone.

'You'll break it then it'll be fucking fucked, won't it?' warned Soap, fighting back.

Bacon, meanwhile, had just been getting on with it.

'It's ringing,' he announced. Eddy and Soap instantly shut the fuck up.

On the bridge, Tom leant over the hand rail to push the guns over the edge. As he did so, his mobile nearly slipped out of his inside coat pocket. Tom took it out and put it in his mouth, holding it between his teeth. Then, holding on to the rail for support, he dangled over the parapet, reaching towards the guns. At full stretch, he was within a inch or two of his goal, but he dared not let go of the rail.

Then Tom's mobile phone began to ring.

His hand at last reached the guns hidden in their bundle of cloth. To answer his phone, Tom had to either drop the guns, or let go of the rail. He froze for a few seconds as the phone continued to ring.

Then he made his decision.